Seeking the Source

Jan Arriens

Illustrated by
Margaret Mence Baker

SERENDIPITY

Copyright © Jan Arriens 2005

First Published in 2005 by

Serendipity
First Floor
37 / 39 Victoria Road
Darlington
DL1 5SF

British Library Cataloguing-in-Publication data
A catalogue record for this book is available from the British Library

ISBN 1-84394-183-X

Printed and bound by CPI Antony Rowe, Eastbourne

To Julian, Elizabeth and Edward

Contents

The Suitor's Task

Once there was an extraordinarily beautiful young princess in India. She was named Savitri. She lived in a big palace, with great curving roofs and a long sloping lawn that stretched down to the street. As a little girl, she would play in the gardens and sometimes go right down to the railings near the street. This in fact was the spot that she liked best. It was so different from her luxurious, comfortable palace life where her every need was attended to. Here, she could watch the hustle and bustle of street life. She would see the ox-drawn carts go by laden with timber and hides and mountains of vegetables. She would watch the street-hawkers scurrying down the street, with two balancing pans at either end of a long pole over their shoulder. Best of all, there was the pancake seller who used to park his little cart just outside the palace fence.

Savitri was not really meant to go down there but there were times when her nurse was busy, or when people were distracted by visitors, or when she was thought to be quietly in her room but managed to slip out. And in fact people didn't really mind, for Savitri was such a lovable little girl and, while curious, never tried to venture beyond the palace gates.

At the fence she would also see sick people and people who couldn't walk properly or others who had lost an arm or a leg. She wondered at the lives they must lead, and wished she could invite them all into the Palace. Often after a banquet there was so much food left over! Sometimes, when the festivities were at their height, she would slip away unnoticed with a pot of rice and vegetables, which she would ladle out through the railings of the fence into the outstretched hands of poor people. As soon as the bowl was empty she would dash inside again with it before anyone noticed - although the poor people noticed!

Often, she would talk to the pancake seller. Now this was the one thing she wasn't meant to do, as he was of much lower caste, but she took no notice of that. He was really little more than a boy, but seemed to have such wisdom. Savitri would ask him about some of the strange people walking by. "Who is that big fat woman with the tired old goat?"

"Ah, that is Nandee," replied Vishnu. "She has a family of fourteen children and sometimes comes to market with something to sell and then buys things for the family. Today she is selling the goat. She lives in a village beside the river two hours' walk away."

Vishnu always seemed to know everything about everyone. Savitri sometimes thought that he was making things up, but it didn't matter, as his stories were always full of warmth, interest and laughter, and taught her so much about the world beyond her gates. She learned of mothers who died in childbirth leaving large families to be looked after by someone else, she learned of hunger and disease and the lives of endless toil that so many people lived. Once she espied a handsome looking soldier in a dashing costume, with a scary, curved sword on his belt. Vishnu said that the soldier had been in a distant battle and had been very brave. Savitri wanted to know all about war.

"Why do people kill each other if they can't agree? That seems a very silly thing to do. How can you be happy if you have had to kill people to get something?"

Here Vishnu had to bite his tongue, for the princess's father, King Raman, was a famous warrior who ruled over a large territory gained in war some years before Savitri was born. The King no longer bothered with wars as he was now very rich and because he had a big army and was greatly feared.

But he also had no answer to her question.

Sometimes Savitri would be caught talking to Vishnu and would be scolded and sent to her room. The worst punishment was when she wasn't allowed out of the Palace into the garden for days in a row. In the distance, at the bottom of the sloping garden, she could just make out Vishnu and his little cart and all the people that she had come to know about and even love.

And then at last she would be allowed out again. If the truth be known, her kindly mother, Queen Pari, liked her girl's adventurous spirit and inquiring mind. So did the King, who knew it was no bad thing for his daughter to see something of the real world: she was their only child, and one day would rule over the land that was now his.

So Savitri went down to the fence again. Sometimes when business was quiet Vishnu would start playing a small wooden flute. He played it most beautifully. In her innocent way Savitri would sing along with the flute, which would lead her into strange and beautiful lands almost as wonderful and magical as the stories Vishnu told her.

One day, when Savitri came back to the Palace, she found the King on the steps. He asked her what she had been doing, and she told him that she had been singing with the pancake seller who, she said, played more beautiful music than any of the court musicians.

The King said that he had heard the faint sound of music on the evening air. He turned gravely to Savitri and said, "My child, you are fourteen now and turning into a young woman. We will be having a ceremony to celebrate your womanhood, and soon people will be coming to ask for your hand in marriage."

"But I don't want to marry!" exclaimed Savitri. "I am much too young." She sobbed so violently that the King reached an agreement with her. "Normally," he said, "your parents would decide whom you should marry, but I am going to let you decide. You must choose wisely. If by the age of eighteen you have still not chosen someone to marry, then I and your mother will do so."

The age of eighteen seemed so far off to Savitri that her cares dropped away. She skipped gaily down to Vishnu to tell him her news. But it was to be the last time she was allowed to speak to him. Soon, almost every day, a suitor - always Princes - would appear at the gates to the Palace asking for the Princess's hand in marriage. Stories of her great beauty and kindness spread far and wide.

News of the Princess spread even further with each new suitor she rejected. It was not that she ever said "No"; instead she would look searchingly at each young - and sometimes not so young - man, as though reading his innermost secrets.

To one she would say, "There is one thing I want you to do and I will take your hand in marriage. I want you to give away all your wealth to poor women struggling to bring up big families by themselves." To another, she would say, "I want you to stop your life of party-going and merry-making and to spend a year in silent meditation in a monastery." Time after time, she would ask something that the suitor was unable to do.

So the years passed. Fewer people came to the Palace now, as all the Princes from far and wide had tried and failed to do what the Princess had asked of them.

One day a very famous Prince from a distant part of India came to the Palace. His name was Srinivas. He arrived at the head of a magnificent procession of 20 cream-coloured elephants with glistening tusks. Their huge wide backs were bedecked with glorious, shimmering silk cloths adorned with emeralds, topaz and pearls. Built on top of the leading elephants were little tentlike houses, and it was from one of these that the Great Prince grandly emerged. Behind the procession was the Prince's army of 20,000 men. Trumpets sounded, peacocks were released into the street, a magnificent red carpet was unrolled all the way up to the Palace.

Confidently and directly, Prince Srinivas strode up to the King. "I would have your daughter's hand in marriage," he said, the sun sparkling on the chain of port-red rubies around his neck. His voice carried effortlessly so that every trader in the market, every servant in the Palace and even every soldier could hear. The King replied gravely, "You must ask my daughter. It is for her to decide."

The Prince repeated his question, making showers of white ibises fly up from the palace turrets and the surrounding trees.

Savitri looked at the Prince evenly. "I know, I know," said the Prince boldly, "there is one thing you would like me to do. Name it, oh most beautiful, most adorable Princess and I shall make you mine."

"There is one thing I want you to do and I will take your hand in marriage," she said quietly but distinctly. "There is a pancake seller just outside the palace fence; you can see him from here. Every day he is there, from dawn until late at night, in the scorching sun and in the driving rain. He never has a holiday, and the little money he earns goes to support the family of which he is the oldest son. I want you to take his place, wearing his clothes, and playing his flute, for just one day so that he can have a rest."

There was a long silence. The only sound was that of the ibises fluttering back into position on the roof and in the trees. Even the sun seemed momentarily to stand still. Beads of sweat formed on the Prince's brow. He opened his mouth as though to speak but then fainted and crashed to the ground.

Cold cloths were applied, fans fluttered and an umbrella was held over the Prince. At length he regained consciousness. He looked strangely at the Princess, got up and went back to his retinue of elephants. Sorrowfully he rode away into the gathering pink and grey dusk.

This time the King could not contain his anger. "You have sent away the most important man in all India with your ridiculous demands. Mercifully you are nearing the age of eighteen so soon it will be possible for me and your mother to choose you a good husband."

The next day was quiet. Many days thereafter were quiet. No more suitors came. People in the Palace left Savitri alone. Much of the time she spent playing music and singing. Then, one day, ignoring the rules, she walked barefoot over the grass down to the railings. It was many years since she had spoken to Vishnu. He was bent over his food cart. He would not look at her. When she spoke to him he did not answer. At length he said, "Surely you must know that I can no longer look on or speak to you."

"Why not?" she said. "These are but customs that we ourselves have laid down, and which we can change. You may look at me, you may talk to me. You are so wise, Vishnu, why does no one ever ask for my hand any more?"

"Because, Princess, there is hardly a Prince in the land who has not been to see you, and those who have not know that they would be unable to perform the task you set them."

"But there are more than just Princes in the world."

"Truly there are, but you can only marry a Prince," replied Vishnu.

"No one has ever said that," said the Princess. "That too is custom."

Vishnu did not sleep that night. The Princess's words went round and round in his head. "No one has ever said that, that too is custom." What did she mean by that? Was it possible - no, it could not be. But the thoughts would not leave him. For days he hardly slept; customers began to complain about his pancakes, because he had left out a vital ingredient or only half-cooked them.

Vishnu left his stall. He marched to the palace gates, where he was surprised to find the King looking impatiently into the distance. "The last day, the last day, her last chance and then we shall be able to choose."

Drawing a strength from he knew not where, Vishnu said as boldly as he was able, "Great King, I would ask for your daughter's hand in marriage." The King looked at the ragged street-vendor in disbelief. "You - you are not a Prince! You are a creature from the gutter, whom I could crush beneath my heel. Be off with you, and count yourself the most fortunate of men that you can mock your King and live to tell the tale."

Then came the Princess's quiet voice. "Father Dear, you never said my suitor had to be a prince. Do please let him approach." Astonished, the King let Vishnu pass. He went up to the Princess. "There is one thing I would like you to do and I will take your hand in marriage," she said looking at him gently.

"I know, I know," he exclaimed before she could go on, "you want me to stand on one leg on top of a column in the market square for a full day and night without moving and eating." And without further ado he ran off to the market square, climbed up on top of the highest column and stood there like a bird with one leg folded back for an entire day and an entire night. The town's people thronged the square, marvelling at Vishnu's stillness until, at last, the day and the night were over. Without so much as pausing to have something to eat, he ran back to the Palace. The Princess was waiting. So was the King. "It is too late. You are eighteen this day. Now your mother and I will choose a husband for you."

"No, dear Father," said the Princess, "I still have one suitor who has not yet performed the task I want of him." Turning to Vishnu she said, "There is one other thing I would like you to do…" "I know, I know," cried Vishnu, "you wish me to clean every cobblestone in the market square with a toothbrush until people could eat off them." And before the Princess could so much as utter another word he had gone.

The market square was cleaned until it dazzled the eyes of those who beheld it. Back Vishnu went to the Princess. Once again she said, "There is one other thing I would like you to do …" and he was gone, this time promising to build a bridge across the river where it was badly needed by the poor country-dwellers who came into the town. Many volunteers came and helped him, and soon the job was done.

And so Vishnu planted trees along the sides of every road leading into the town. He painted the houses of those who could not afford to do so themselves. He baked bread for thousands. He spent a year in a monastery not uttering a word. He fasted from one new moon to the next, until people came from all over India to marvel at him. He built a school and a temple and a hospital.

Each time the Princess would once again say, "There is one other thing I would like you to do …" and Vishnu would perform some other extraordinary task of his own invention. Nothing seemed enough, but Vishnu was clever enough never to let the Princess ask him to perform the one task which, seeing through him, she knew he would be unable to perform. All the while, the Princess insisted that as Vishnu had still not performed the task she wanted, she was still not released from her right to choose her suitor.

Vishnu began to run out of things to do. His imagination could no longer stretch to what he thought might please the Princess and make her change her mind. He came before the Princess again. "There is one other thing I would like you to do," she began but before she could finish her question, he exclaimed "I will roll all the way to the holy city of Benares and back."

Now Benares was 300 miles away. Rolling so fast he was almost a blur, Vishnu rolled to Benares and back in just twenty days. Surely now the Princess would not doubt his love and devotion. Exhausted, he rolled slowly past where the elephants had stood and the trumpets had sounded and to the spot where his stall used to stand and where there was now just a collapsed heap of little planks. His body could remember every stone on the way to and the way from Benares. His skin bore the mark of every twig and thorn he had rolled over. The sun, the moon, clouds, rain, thunder, mist, ice, puddles and hills coursed about in his brain until, like the Great Prince, he fainted.

Savitri was there. As Vishnu regained consciousness, he heard her saying, distantly and as though in a dream, "There is one thing I would like you to do and I will take your hand in marriage." He wanted to get up, he wanted to interrupt her and dash off, but he could not. It was all he could do to open his eyes and hear what she said.

"I want you to accept my love for you."

The Dance in the Dew

The day dawned fair. Normally, before a great event in the royal household, the beautiful white ibises that had made the Palace their home would circle around in their hundreds, unable to settle down because of all the noise and activity. But today all was quiet, even though it was the day on which Princess Savitri was to marry Vishnu, the pancake seller.

"We shall have the best food, the best wines, orchestras, magicians, acrobats, dancers and singers!" said King Raman. "It will be a day our country will never forget."

"At last, at last," said Queen Pari, "our daughter is getting married. I think Vishnu must have been a prince in a former life and has come to earth again to win our dear daughter."

The King and Queen had both found it difficult to accept that their beautiful daughter was to marry someone of such lowly origin. But they loved their daughter dearly and had learned to respect her strange determination to do things her own way. It was as though she had a sixth sense to guide her.

And so it was that Princess Savitri, with Vishnu by her side, said, "No, Father, we shall not be having a grand wedding. It will be a day of celebration but we would like it to be as simple as possible."

"As simple as possible?" said the King in astonishment. "But this is a unique day. We must do all in our power to make it memorable."

"Let Vishnu explain," said Savitri quietly.

"Well, your great Highness," Vishnu began hesitantly. "You see, not long ago I was selling pancakes in a stall by the fence just outside the Palace gates. My friends – well, they are the people of the streets. They are poor, but they are honest. How when I already have such happiness could I allow such sums of money to be spent that they can only dream of? It would not be fair to them and, besides, it would not add so much as an ibis's feather to my happiness or that of your dear daughter."

"But what will you do to mark the day?" exclaimed the King. "There must be music and there must be pageantry! Drums must roll, trumpets must sound, soldiers must march

in their scarlet and black uniforms! Our guests from far and wide must go home impressed by our wealth, generosity and excellent organisation. They must see that we are a country not to be trifled with. And we must celebrate, we must celebrate!"

"Father dear, we want you to tell all the rich and important visitors whom you have invited that we shall be giving all the money saved to the poor. So many people in our country have so little. They have suffered from disease, flood, fire, famine, earthquake and, until recently, war. Now that our country has known greater prosperity and peace than it has for many years, we must share this with everyone we can."

"And," said Vishnu, growing bolder, "the people will sing and dance and make music! They will wear the finest clothes they have. Their happiness and rejoicing will be our celebration. All we must do is provide them with food - honest, plain, simple food."

The King and the Queen were silent. What could they say? The country had seen how the Princess had rejected a long line of suitors, setting tasks which she knew they could not perform. The people loved her for this, and they also loved Vishnu for daring to ask for her hand. At length the King said:

"It shall be as you say. Sometimes we must not plan our path in life but let it unfold before us. It is not what I would want but let us see what happens. We can always have a grand official ceremony in a year's time when you are more aware of your duties of state."

So it was that the only sounds of activity on the morning of the wedding came from the great kitchens of the palace, where tureens of soup and mounds of fragrant rice were being prepared. People had slept overnight outside the Palace railings. All over the city, men, women and children emerged gorgeously attired from their drab little lean-to dwellings. How such poor people could produce such spotlessly clean and well-pressed apparel in the midst of all their squalor and dust was a source of astonishment to the many important visitors who had come from far-off parts.

All morning long the ordinary people of the town filed in through the Palace gates. They brought with them no presents - for Savitri and Vishnu had insisted that there should be none - but they came with gold and silver flags, and streamers and ribbons in the deepest of blues and most delicate of pinks. They wore flowers in their hair and scattered rose petals before them.

Above all, they brought simple musical instruments: bamboo flutes such as Vishnu himself played, hour-glass drums, little wooden blocks with small metal jingles mounted in them, and simple lutes made from a gourd and a length of bamboo. Little groups of musicians teamed up and the people played and sang and danced until the sun was going down.

All the while the kitchen produced a steady flow of food. To feed the many thousands great tureens of soup were poured into the basin around the Grand Fountain, which had been specially emptied and cleaned for the purpose, so that people could scoop up servings with the containers they had brought with them. Huge barrels of rice were served which, however much people dipped in their containers, never seemed to empty.

At first the important people from distant parts of India looked uncomfortable; there was no present-giving ceremony, no occasion for the beautifully dressed women to show off their finery, no elegant, formal dances, no performances of plays, no speeches or opportunities to display wealth and importance. But slowly they began to mingle with the ordinary people and to take a delight in the simple music and to walk like everyone else around the the magnificent Palace grounds, where the Princess and Vishnu were mixing with as many people as they could.

Just before the sun set, the King climbed to the top of the marble steps in front of the Palace and held up his arms. People gathered round and fell silent.

"Honoured guests and dear people of my country, I have just one thing to say to you. I have seen how you hold my dear daughter and her new husband in such affection. You have seen how it was her determination that led to her choice of husband, and now you have seen the way in which they have chosen to celebrate, with such simplicity. Truly, they are in touch with the people of this land.

"To mark our happiness on this day and out of respect for this wisdom, Queen Pari and I have decided that from this day on we shall no longer be King and Queen but that Vishnu and Savitri shall rule over you."

The King's voice echoed against the palace walls and in the trees in the stillness of the fading day. For some moments there was silence. Then Nandee - the poor woman seen by Savitri through the Palace railings as a girl as she went to market to sell her old goat - cried out, "Long live King Vishnu and Queen Savitri!" Thousands of voices rose like one into the evening sky.

****

Savitri and Vishnu loved one another deeply. It was as though they knew each other's innermost thoughts. To begin with they ruled wisely and well. Instead of spending money on armies and outward display, the new King and Queen carefully made sure that those in need were not forgotten.

One day it was announced that the Grand Sultan of the neighbouring land of Koh-i-Noor was to visit. He was a ruler with a mighty army and a short temper. He loved finery and pageantry. He had sent his ambassador, the Grand Plenipotentiary Extraordinary, to discuss arrangements for the visit. King Vishnu and Queen Savitri decided to consult King Raman about what to do.

"I know you do not like ceremony and pomp," said the former King. "But the Grand Sultan is a proud and dangerous man. It would be unwise to create an enemy of him. He will want to be received with due respect and pageantry. There must be a red carpet, a Guard of Honour and a military band. You must hold a banquet and a ball. There must be fireworks and a jousting tournament."

"No," said Vishnu. "We shall assemble the best scholars in the land to give learned discourses. We will take the Grand Sultan on a tour of our botanical gardens and row him up the river to show him the bridges and flood defences we have built. We shall get ordinary people in from the city to perform folk dances and folk songs. Then truly he will understand our country."

King Raman replied that they would be making a grave mistake, for the Grand Sultan would be offended. Now Savitri and Vishnu loved the old King and knew that his advice was not given lightly. But they could not go against everything they stood for, and told the Grand Plenipotentiary Extraordinary what they proposed to do.

"Your gracious Majesties," the Grand Plenipotentiary Extraordinary said carefully, "my Master is a great and powerful ruler. He comes to pay his respects, but will wish you to pay yours in return. He intends conveying magnificent gifts and has asked me to arrange a feast for a thousand people to last for three days and three nights. He will be bringing all the notables of his land and wishes to sign a Treaty of Peace for all time between our two lands. When he comes to you in such a spirit of generosity I fear for what may happen if his Gracious Presence is not honoured in that same spirit."

Vishnu and Savitri consulted with King Raman until long in the night. Their candles had burned right down when at last they returned to the Grand Plenipotentiary Extraordinary. He was asleep, exhausted, his sword still buckled to his belt as he lay back in the rich silk cushions on the sofa.

Gently Vishnu shook him by the shoulder and the Grand Plenipotentiary Extraordinary woke up. "The programme shall be as you want," said Vishnu. "We agree to respect our honoured guest's wishes."

The visit was a success. It provided a spectacle such as had not been seen for many years within the Palace walls. Much of the Kingdom's wealth, held for an emergency in the form of gold and silver jewellery and gemstones in two great metal chests, was used up. Where once the chests had been full to overflowing, now the bottom could be seen.

The Grand Sultan departed and the Treaty of Peace was signed.

But many people in the Royal Council, which Savitri and Vishnu had set up to help rule the country, were unhappy. They grumbled that so much money had been spent on visiting foreigners while their own pay was so low and they never had any fine ceremonies to look forward to at which they could wear their Royal Councillors' robes. There was whispering against Vishnu and Savitri behind their backs. The Council divided into factions. A vote was taken and it was agreed that their pay should be greatly increased. To give thanks, it was agreed that there would be an annual Royal Pageant of Celebration, with parades and festivals.

The Royal Council also wanted greater powers. In order to improve the country's standing abroad, it was insisted that Queen Savitri and King Vishnu should make visits to neighbouring countries, including mountainous Koh-i-Noor. As their duties became more and more formal and they found themselves having to dress up and give receptions and sign proclamations and treaties, Savitri and Vishnu became more and more unhappy and even began quarrelling. One day Savitri criticised Vishnu for the clothes he was wearing, saying they were not grand enough for the occasion, while he snapped, saying that it set a bad example for her to walk barefoot through the gardens for all to see.

As they became busier they spoke to one another less and less. There was always some ceremony to attend, events to plan, papers to sign. The Royal Council became more and more difficult to deal with.

One morning Savitri, deeply unhappy, went to see Vishnu. He was surrounded by courtiers and piles of paper to read and sign. To Vishnu's mounting anger, Savitri dismissed all the officials. When they were alone, Vishnu exploded with rage. "Can you not see, woman, that there is a mountain of work to do? You cannot come bursting in and disturb these important consultations."

Savitri wept quietly. "Do you not know that today is the anniversary of our betrothal? It was on this day that you came back after rolling all that way and that at last I could stop you from undertaking yet another task and tell you what I had been wanting to say all along. Can you have forgotten what that was?"

There was a long silence. A purple and gold butterfly came in through the window and alighted on the table between them.

"That is like the butterflies you used to follow in your garden as a child when you came down to my stall at the railings," said Vishnu.

"And you would play your flute to me."

Wordlessly Vishnu went over to the cupboard. Opening a drawer he took out his bamboo *venu*. Vishnu blew off the dust and put the small instrument to his lips. Sounds they had not heard for many years came forth. Together they passed out through the door onto the Palace terrace with Vishnu still playing. They came to the flight of steps at the head of which King Raman had announced he was standing down as King. In the shafts of early morning sunlight slanting through the tall trees they descended the stairs. As they came to the long sloping lawns with the dew drops sparkling like diamonds Savitri kicked off her shoes and, as Vishnu continued to play, a little faster and less sadly now, broke into a slight skip. Vishnu too quickened his pace, weaving this way and that and spinning round in circles. Savitri took him by the hand and together they skipped down to the Palace railings.

There was a gap in the railings where they could get through. The little pile of collapsed planks that had once been Vishnu the pancake-seller's stall was still there, now a shrine to the man who had risen from nothing to become King. From other stall holders – the sandal maker, the basket weaver and the ropemaker - Vishnu borrowed a hammer, saw and some nails.

All morning, with Savitri's help, he rebuilt his stand.

This time he made it a little bigger, to take two people.

The River of Life

There was great rejoicing and also astonishment when Vishnu and Savitri stopped being King and Queen and returned to the pancake seller's stall. People flocked to their stall to buy pancakes made by royal hand but, more particularly, just to see them. Mothers came with their children. "Look, there are the King and Queen, who are people just like us!"

Vishnu and Savitri were very happy in their stall and asked Raman if he would ascend to the throne again so that they could stop being King and Queen. King Raman agreed and Vishnu and Savitri moved to a little house outside the Palace not far from their stall. Several years later there were three small children, a girl called Tusti (meaning peace and happiness), a boy called Loprakesh (which means light of the world), and a girl called Ekta (meaning unity). Often they would be at the stall, sometimes sneaking through the gap in the railings to play with other children on the Palace lawns, and sometimes helping their parents in the stall (or getting in the way!). Soon the stall had to be made bigger, with a low counter so that three giggling faces could serve pancakes to other children.

Their grandmother, Queen Pari, would come to the stall most days with little treats for the children and to tell them stories under the spreading flame tree with its gorgeous scarlet flowers and lacey, fernlike leaves. Every now and then their grandfather, King Raman, would come to see them too but, as he was King again, he was very busy and did not have much time.

King Raman had once been a warlike king with a great army who was greatly feared by neighbouring rulers. But as he had got older he had lost interest in fighting and, besides, his country had a permanent Peace Treaty with Koh-i-Noor, the only land that was a possible threat.

Now Koh-i-Noor – the "mountain of light" - was a mountainous country and it was there that the river which ran through the Kingdom of Prithura had its source. It was called the Great River or, after it entered Prithura, the River of Life, and ran all the way to the sea.

One day King Raman came to the stall. He greeted Tusti, Loprakesh and Ekta gravely and said that he needed to speak to Savitri and Vishnu. They put the three children in charge of the stall (watched over by Queen Pari).

"What I have to tell you is very serious," said the King. "I have heard that the Grand Sultan of Koh-i-Noor intends to build a huge dam to provide water for farmers in his country. It means that our river will be blocked off and reduced to a trickle. Our people will face ruin."

"But he cannot do that," said Vishnu. "That would be an act of war. It would be forbidden under our Peace Treaty."

"No," replied the King. "It is not covered by the Treaty. I have only two choices: to go to war or to appeal to the Grand Sultan in a spirit of friendship. Since I no longer have a strong army, and it would take too long and be too costly to raise one, I must go to Koh-i-Noor to talk with him."

"But father," said Savitri, "you have never trusted the Grand Sultan. How could you be sure that he would keep his word?"

"I could not," said the King sadly, "but it is all I can do. I must appeal to his better nature and ask him to be reasonable."

"We shall go with you!" exclaimed Vishnu. But King Raman insisted that he should go alone, with just a few soldiers from the Palace as escort. "Then if anything happens to me you'll have to leave the pancake stall and become King and Queen again. The people love you and you will lead them wisely."

All their pleading was in vain; King Raman set off for the mountainous neighbouring sultanate. Savitri and Vishnu continued as usual in their stall, but every day looked anxiously down the northern road to see if the King was returning.

At last, one day they saw a small cloud of dust on the road in the distance. Savitri and Vishnu left their stall and ran down the road. It was indeed the King. His face was dirty and his hair dusty, and his clothes stained. He looked even older than he was. Tears left streaks in the grime on his face.

"I have made matters worse," he said sorrowfully. "The Grand Sultan was enraged, saying that I had insulted him."

"Whatever did you say, Father Dear?" asked Savitri. "I cannot imagine that you gave offence."

"The Grand Sultan said that the people in the plains of

his country had been suffering from drought and that it was a terrible thing for me to ask him not to give water to his own people. He was so angry that he chased me out of his land, saying that he would be coming soon with a great army to teach me and all Prithura a lesson."

"What did you say then?" asked Vishnu quietly.

"Why, what could I say? I said that I now had only a small army and could do little to stop him, but that he could never win the hearts and minds of the people."

Later Vishnu took Savitri aside. "I fear our dear King has been tricked," he said. "The Grand Sultan would never waste his money and effort on a dam for poor people he despises. But he knew that the rumours would alarm the King and now he knows that we have no army to speak of and cannot defend ourselves."

It was as Vishnu had said. Reports began reaching Prithura that a large army was gathering in Koh-i-Noor. King Raman summoned the Queen, the Royal Council, Savitri and Vishnu and many other important people. "I have made a mistake in allowing our army to run down so that we could spend our money on other things that seemed more important. But our people have no quarrel with the people of Koh-i-Noor. It is I and the Grand Sultan who are at odds. I shall ride out to meet the army and challenge him to battle myself. There is no need for other blood to be shed."

Again the people pleaded with him, saying that there were plenty of strong young men in Prithura and that a mighty army could soon be formed. It might not be well-trained but it would be loyal and determined and could put up a great fight. But King Raman would have none of it. "I have seen enough bloodshed in my time," he said. "Let me go forth and do battle alone. If I die in the eve of my life it will be no great loss, while if fate is with me and I succeed then thousands of lives will be spared." And even though Queen Pari was in tears and begged him not to go, he buckled on his sword, mounted his great black steed and was gone. Not even the soldiers of the Palace Guard were allowed to accompany him.

Two days later King Raman found himself in a wide, lush valley beside the Great River where he found the massed enemy army. A scout rode out to meet him.

"Who goes there!" he demanded.

"I am Raman, King of Prithura. Tell your master that my people have no quarrel with his, but that even as I speak a mighty army is being formed in my land. Let us avoid all this terrible bloodshed by just the two of us doing battle."

The scout rode back. Seated on his magnificent white stallion and dressed in his flowing green robes, the Grand Sultan waited to hear the message brought back by the scout. "Ha!" he exclaimed. "The King has no army, it is a bluff. But it will be the last trick he tries to play on me! He and I shall fight."

A look of contempt stole over the faces of some of the Grand Sultan's soldiers as they watched their leader accept the challenge from the stooped, pathetic figure of the ancient King. Some even turned away as they could not bear to watch.

"It will be a fight to the death," said the King. "You must give me your word that if I am killed none of my people will be harmed. This quarrel is between you and me, and you and me alone."

"Agreed," said the Grand Sultan.

The old King fought magnificently. Summoning his last strength and drawing on all his former skills as a horseman and warrior, he parried the Grand Sultan's blows and ducked and weaved, spinning his horse this way and that, and even managing to land some blows on the Grand Sultan's shoulder plates. But he was too old and lacking in strength. Although the Grand Sultan was himself unable to land so much as a single blow on the King, he managed at last to give the King's horse a sharp blow on the bottom with the flat of his sword. The horse reared up and galloped off into the distance, stopping only when it came to the river, where the King was thrown off. He lay winded on the ground, his ankle twisted. Local villagers ran up to assist him. The King struggled to his feet for the final battle, only to see the Grand Sultan waving on his army and riding off towards Prithura.

On the way the Grand Sultan and his army laid waste to villages, plundering whatever took their fancy. Columns of smoke rose in the air and people fled before the advancing army. As the army approached the Palace the town was deserted. Riding proudly and fearlessly at the head of his army, the Grand

Sultan came to the Palace gates which, to his astonishment, were not even closed. Fearing an ambush, he looked around.

To his even greater astonishment, he saw a man and a woman and three children in a nearby wooden stall, frying pancakes. Motioning six or so of his finest soldiers to ride up to the stall with him, the Grand Sultan approached the couple. Nowhere else was there anyone to be seen (although, had he but known it, several hundred eyes were observing him from behind the sacking and coarse curtains of the shanty dwellings across the road).

The Grand Sultan stopped in front of the stall. His Commander-in-Chief drew up beside him. He nudged the Grand Sultan gently, saying, "You realise who..."

"Do you not show respect to your new King?" thundered the Grand Sultan. Somewhere, in the cave of memory, he recognised the face before him, but could not quite place it. The woman was also strangely familiar. Her face went pale and she said, "Does that mean that King Raman is dead?"

"No," said the Grand Sultan. "But he has been roundly defeated in battle. I demand that you humble yourselves before your new King."

"If you mean that my dear father is no longer King, then Vishnu cannot bow before himself," said Savitri quietly.

The Grand Sultan started. "You ... you ... you are Princess Savitri and ..."

"I am Vishnu. But you are my guest, and please, I would like you to have something to eat and drink."

The Grand Sultan was speechless with amazement. Did this man not realize he could cut off his head with a single blow of his sword? "These are said to be the finest pancakes in the land," said the pancake seller calmly. "I have had many years' practice. Come, I shall feed you and as many of your men as I can. You must be tired and hungry." And he held out a steaming apple pancake before the Grand Sultan.

The wonderful aroma was so enticing that, as if in a dream, the Grand Sultan took the pancake and began to eat. He realised how hungry he was. He had a second, and a third, washing them down with the delicate tea prepared by Savitri. The Commander-in-Chief and the other soldiers also had their fill.

"The Palace gates are open," said Vishnu kindly, "and food has been prepared for your army. Let me take you to your quarters in the Palace; you must bring in your soldiers."

As they walked towards the Palace gates people streamed out of their little huts, cheering, "Long live dear Vishnu! Long live dear Savitri!" The Grand Sultan looked angrily at Vishnu. He was about to complain that no-one was shouting out his name when he felt someone take him by the hand. It was Tusti.

Skipping, the little girl drew him through the Palace gates. As they walked up the long drive to the Palace, she tugged the Grand Sultan this way and that, showing him the Indian Red Admiral and Striped Tiger butterflies on some bushes, and a secret pond tucked away behind a stand of bamboo.

Suddenly she disappeared behind a bush. "Can't catch me!" Tusti cried. The Grand Sultan dashed after her. It was a bit undignified, but he couldn't allow himself to be outsmarted by a mere child. Loprakesh and Ekta joined in the game. Every time he caught one of the children they had to stand still and could only move again when one of the other children touched them. "I'll catch all three of you!" the Grand Sultan shouted. Sometimes he managed to turn two of the children into statues but he never quite succeeded in tagging all three. At last, tired out, the Grand Sultan lay down on the grass laughing. He hadn't enjoyed himself so much in years.

Later that night, after a fine dinner on the terrace beneath the full moon, the Grand Sultan sat back contentedly. Life was good. The only irritation was that pesky pancake seller. The Grand Sultan muttered when alone to the Commander-in-Chief, "Who does he think he is, this man from the gutter, to treat me with so little fear?"

The Commander-in-Chief replied cautiously, "Well, Your Highness, he is after all now King."

"He is nothing of the kind! I am the King! Once a pancake seller always a pancake seller!"

That night the Grand Sultan did not sleep well. He was tired from all the running around, but lay awake, tossing and turning, angry and bewildered. Here he was, after so courageously defeating King Raman in single-handed combat and having brought his entire army to the capital city without the loss of so much as a single man, and all he needed to do now was to deal with this upstart pancake seller. If he could just get rid of him, the Kingdom would be his and his alone. Something else was bothering him too, but he wasn't quite sure what.

He could not help thinking of Vishnu's calm and kind manner as he had served the pancakes and of the three giggling little faces behind the counter. What could have made a man of such humble origins turn his back on the biggest prize the Kingdom of Prithura had to offer? Why would he give up the fine clothes, the riches, the banquets, the servants and all the power and glory of being King to become a mere stallholder again? But the people loved him, that was clear. Such people were dangerous.

Next morning, the Grand Sultan and Commander-in-Chief breakfasted alone in the morning room, with its great windows, flanked by heavy velvet curtains, overlooking the terrace and gardens. As they were eating their mango and melon, the Grand Sultan announced, "This man Vishnu is much loved by the people. That could cause us much harm. I have decided that he must be executed."

There was a movement in the corner of the room. Out from behind the curtains came a little figure. It was Tusti, followed by Loprakash and Ekta, who had been hiding there. The Grand Sultan and Commander-in-Chief looked startled. Tusti sprang up on the Grand Sultan's knee. "What does executed mean?" She tried to look at the Grand Sultan, but he looked away. She grabbed him by the gold braiding on his uniform with her little hands. "What does it mean?" And she put her face right up to his so that he could not look away.

"It means," said the Grand Sultan hesitantly and after some thought, "that he is to go on a long journey. He will be going to another land."

"Is that what it really means?" said Tusti in a very small voice. "I thought – I thought that it meant that someone had to die."

The Grand Sultan was silent. At length he felt a little figure tugging at his flowing royal robe. It was Ekta. She pulled so hard at his garment that he was forced to look at her. "Do you mean my daddy has to die?" she asked, with big round eyes. Meanwhile, out of the corner of his eye, the Grand Sultan saw Loprakesh standing there looking very sad and frightened but standing up straight like a little soldier.

Many thoughts went through the Grand Sultan's mind at once. He had visions of a grand battle, a victory parade and a magnificent coronation ceremony when he would be proclaimed master of two great lands. His name would be feared far and wide. He would have the biggest army in all India. At the same time he was thinking how the man he was intending to execute wasn't even interested in being king but seemed to have an inner peace from just being himself. He looked at the three children; the three pairs of eyes were like beams of light that shone straight into his heart. He fidgeted, he looked this way and that, sweat broke out on his brow. Several times he tried to speak but for a long time no words would come.

"In my country," he said at last, "in my country it means - it also means to show that someone is special. Yes, that is what it means. Forgive me, dear children, but I must go. There is something I need to do."

Giving orders to the Commander-in-Chief to withdraw the army and return to Koh-i-Noor, the Grand Sultan took leave of Queen Pari, Vishnu and Savitri and in turn lifted up the three children and kissed them gravely on the cheek. "You must all come and stay with me some time," he said. "I will show you the butterflies in my land and we can play hide-and-seek in my Palace!"

With that the Grand Sultan strode out of the morning room, over the terrace, down the steps and along the path to the Palace gates. Soldiers from his army rushed up to his side to escort him, but he sent them away with a quick word. All by himself, he struck down the long dusty road out of town.

All day and all night the Grand Sultan strode on. At last, on the second day, he espied in the distance what he had been looking for. Coming towards him was an old man. His clothes were dusty and he had a limp. He and the Grand Sultan met one another at a bend of the river as the sun was at its highest.

The Grand Sultan kneeled down in the dust before the raggedy man. "Great King Raman," he began, but no more words came. He remained on one knee, with the King stooped over him. All nature seemed to stand still. Then King Raman went to the bank of the river, scooped up some water and held out his hands for the Grand Sultan to drink from the River of Life.

Seeking the Source

They struggled up the hill. The path was well-defined, but was getting ever narrower and steeper. They could hear the screech of monkeys, and strange, haunting cries of unfamiliar birds. Below them the chalk-coloured river tumbled and boiled down the hillside with a great roar.

"Just keep going until you reach the great outcrop of rock," the innkeeper had said. "You will see the cave - you cannot miss it."

The trees were thinning out a little as they climbed higher, but were still too lush and tall for the two travellers to see where they were going.

"You must call on one of the holy men," the innkeeper in the small market town high up in the hills had insisted. "You can't possibly climb up to the source of the Great River without visiting one of the hermits."

After Vishnu and Savitri had decided to get married they discovered that there was an ancient tradition in Prithura for new couples to journey to the source of the Great River before the birth of their first child. The tradition had long died out but, sensing perhaps the spirit of their ancestors, they too had decided there was no better way to start their married life than to find the dawn of the great life-giving source of water. This meant travelling to the land of Koh-i-Noor, the Mountain of Light.

As children they had been told stories at their mother's knee about the Great River. Vishnu had drawn water from the river with his mother, while Savitri had scattered hibiscus blossom into it with the Queen to bless the poor; they had learned to swim in the river; they had floated candles down it at religious festivals; and they knew it as a great commercial artery, with its fishing boats, sailing vessels, barges and other flat-bottomed craft. They knew how, further downstream, it could burst its banks when the snows melted or after the rains, spreading precious silt over the land but sometimes also flooding with great loss of life. It was a river that had a life of its own and a story to tell, a river of legend and ritual, a river of mystery and hopes and fears, a river to be respected, to be admired and above all to be cherished and loved.

King Raman had insisted that they travel the first part of

the journey by elephant. Vishnu had protested: "I am just a poor pancake seller, and unaccustomed to such riches and luxury. I would much rather go on foot." But the King would have none of it. "You are a prince now. You cannot disappoint the people. They want to cheer you as you pass through their villages with your bride on top of Kurgan, the finest elephant in the land."

"But please, Your Highness," begged Vishnu, "don't tell the Sultan of Koh-i-Noor that we are coming. Otherwise everyone will make a great fuss over us. We just want to climb the great mountain like anyone else." The King reluctantly agreed.

And so it was that Savitri and Vishnu found themselves swaying high above the ground on top of Kurgan, the magnificent 70-year old royal elephant. As the king had foretold, vast crowds appeared in every village to cheer them on their way, casting rose petals in the path of the great swaying beast.

At length they entered the Kingdom of Koh-i-Noor, climbing slowly into the foothills to the mighty snow-clad mountains in which the Great River had its source. The path gradually moved away from the river. They could see the water glinting in the distance in the late afternoon sun. Then the river was lost to sight and only the line of trees on the horizon still told where it was. Trees with wonderful yellow and crimson flowers began to enfold the track, gradually forming a green tunnel that scraped over Kurgan's head and along the roof of their purple canopy. The bends in the road became ever sharper, patches of moss began to appear on the rocks and little streams of water ran off the hillsides, cascading onto the road in tiny waterfalls.

"It's getting cooler!" exclaimed Savitri. There was a freshness in the air: not an evening freshness, but the freshness of tumbling water and gathering mists. "Look – the black wet rocks are just like dog's noses!" she said merrily. She wrapped her deep blue sari more closely around her and snuggled up to Vishnu. He wrapped his cloak around her shoulder and, with his other hand, pointed down into the valley where, far below, wisps of smoke could be seen rising from the little houses as people prepared the evening meal. From time to time they would pass a shrine or richly coloured temple.

At last, just as it was growing dark, they reached the small town of Rikash. Just outside the town, Savitri and Vishnu climbed down from the elephant, telling the keeper to take

Kurgan back to Prithura. They would proceed on foot. Savitri hugged the enormous creature by the trunk.

Thin-sounding bells chimed in the distance. In the town they found an inn, where they were warmly received by the innkeeper. At least here in Koh-i-Noor nobody knew who they were and they could pass themselves off as just a young newly married couple.

"It is so wonderful that you are making this journey," the innkeeper said. "In my parents' time it was still quite a common thing to do, but now people no longer make the pilgrimage."

"Well," said Vishnu, "I'm not quite sure that it's a pilgrimage. I'm not very sure about all the religious trappings, you know, but the river has played such a big part in our lives that I would be fascinated to see where it begins its life in the mountains."

"Don't worry," Savitri added hastily, "it means much more to me. I love all the ancient legends about the mountains and am longing to meet some of the holy men who live here." Vishnu had pretended to pull a wry face, and it was then that the innkeeper had insisted that they should call on one of the hermits. "In the morning I will show you and kind lady the path you need to follow. That will take you to the lookout known as the Footprint of the Lord Vishnu, where there is sure to be a holy man to give you a blessing for your own footprints as you climb the mountain up to the source of the Great River."

In the morning, at the innkeeper's advice, they bought some dried fruits – a great luxury - and mangoes in the market. "It is the custom to bring the hermits some food, which they will then bless and share with you." Then, more heavily laden than they would have liked, they trudged along the narrow path between the lush hills until they reached the vantage point, where they had a magnificent view of the mountains ahead and the valleys and plains below. Strange old holy men in orange robes, the sadhus, were sitting about meditating or reading religious texts and counting beads. As the innkeeper had predicted, one of these provided them with a blessing for the journey, daubing coloured pigments on their foreheads.

"All this is such nonsense," said Vishnu as they walked away and were out of earshot. "All these silly rituals. Why on earth will we have a better journey because someone has stuck sticky paint between our eyes?"

Savitri laughed. "You take things much too literally, dear Vishnu," she said. "People need symbols and little ways of doing things. It is not the rituals themselves that matter, but the meaning behind them. And I know you sense the meaning!"

Now it was Vishnu's turn to laugh. "How well you know me already! But I think I will be happier when we are up in the mountains away from all the hustle and bustle."

They returned from the viewpoint and rejoined the track beside the river. At this point the Great River was still wide and impressive, although here it flowed a good deal more quickly than in the plains around Prithura. In a clearing between the trees they came across a family of red-bottomed monkeys, which scampered off, chattering madly. They reached a bend in the river where it was joined by another, smaller river. Now, the Great River river was much less wide, with rocks and even the occasional rapids. It rushed along with a roar, the water chalky and peppermint-coloured.

The air grew cooler and the path slightly steeper. Savitri suggested that they stop for lunch. "My pack is getting heavier and heavier!" she exclaimed. "It's all those dried apricots, sultanas and almonds. My feet are getting sore already and how my legs are aching!"

Vishnu was too proud to admit that he too was beginning to tire. His pack was heavier than Savitri's, and he was dripping with perspiration. Here, the path was still rising gently. It would soon grow steeper. There was still such a long way to go. He began to think of comfortable chairs, soft beds, a hot bath and a change of clothes. Even the thought of standing at his steaming pancake stall on a hot day was appealing.

Later in the day, they came to a rocky ravine. The river was flowing faster now, hissing along and bubbling and dancing around the rocks. After a while the ravine became too steep and rocky to follow the course of the river. A path led away from the water and up the side of the cliff. Here and there steps had been cut into the side of the hill, but even so it was slow and heavy going. Vishnu was secretly glad when Savitri kept stopping at ever shorter intervals to get back her breath.

At last they reached the top of the cliff, where all at once they found themselves on a kind of plateau. Lower down, it had seemed that there was no wind at all, but here on the exposed high plain the wind was rushing up the mountain and they suddenly felt cold. There were far fewer trees now, and such as there were were stunted and bent by the continual winds.

As evening fell they at last saw the rock face they had been told about, with its dark caves like so many blind eyes. A curl of smoke could be seen emerging from one of the black holes. Beyond that stretched the mountain with, somewhere, the source of the river.

But in fact it was Savitri who kept going steadily with quiet determination, while Vishnu longed for her to stop for a rest. There was nowhere to shelter on the ridge and they knew they had to press on for the caves.

They reached the caves as the sun was setting. Just as they were wondering what they should do, a man emerged from one of them. He had a long white beard and was dressed in an ankle-length, flowing robe of unbleached cotton. He folded his hands together and inclined his head towards them. Vishnu and Savitri returned the greeting.

"Welcome," said the holy man, "You have arrived just in time. It gets cold quickly when the sun goes down. Please - you must spend the night in my cave."

He was, he said, called Hemadri. "The name means mountain of gold," he explained, pointing to the mountains with a sweep of his hand. Vishnu and Savitri gasped. Until now they had been trudging along the ridge, heads down, concentrating on each step. Only now did they truly take in the vista in front of them.

Timeless, mysterious, awe-inspiring, the ancient mountains enclosed them in a vast semicircle: great sentinels of light, their rock faces and glaciers afire in the setting sun.

"Oh, it's still such a long way to go, Vishnu!" said Savitri at length. "I am so afraid I am going to let you down."

"You do indeed still have a long way to go," said Hemadri. "Although it depends which way you go. There are many paths up the mountain."

"Just like people say that all the different religions are different paths up the same mountain," said Savitri brightly.

"I prefer," said the sage, "to think that the great religions are all the same path up different mountains."

Vishnu looked puzzled. "How can we all be on the same path but on different mountains?"

"We are all seeking the source, just as you are now. Our circumstances differ, that is all," said the mountain dweller. "It is also a path that has no end but, which once begun, has ended. But come - you must rest and have something to eat."

Savitri and Vishnu conferred hastily. Was this hermit one of the holy men the innkeeper had mentioned? Should they share their dried fruits with him?

As though reading their minds, Hemadri said, "If you have any special food, save it for the Master who lives in a hut further up the main track. The ascent is steep but not difficult, and the weather is set fair. The Master's hut would be a good place for you to stay the night tomorrow before you make your final ascent to the source of the Great River. He is a true muni – a silent yogi."

"But what can we learn from him if he doesn't speak?" asked Vishnu.

"We will learn just from being in his presence," said Savitri quietly. "And I am sure we can learn a lot from you, revered master, living here all by yourself in this remote place."

"Oh no," said Hemadri. "I am no master. When I came here I brought no possessions except for holy books and was sure I would become very wise, as I would have so much time to contemplate their meaning and to meditate. But the longer I am here, the less I know that I know."

"What – what do you know?" asked Vishnu.

"What do I know?" said Hemadri slowly, accepting some rice and dried fish they had brought. He stirred the ingredients together with some spices in a pot on the open fire near the mouth of the cave. Vishnu and Savitri gratefully huddled close to the fire, feeling the warmth return to their limbs. For a long time the holy man was silent. "What do I know? Only that life is awareness."

"Awareness of what?" Vishnu asked, after a pause.

"Of the mystery - that is all."

"What mystery?"

"The mystery that is with us all the time."

"And where do we find this mystery you speak of?" persisted Vishnu.

"Here, in the mountains around us, in serving other people, or inside you, in meditation."

"Whenever I try meditating it just seems empty and boring. I would rather marvel at the thunderclouds or listen to the singing of the birds or smell the sweet scent of frangipani blossom in the cool of the morning," replied Vishnu.

"All these things you can find in the silence too. Let your strivings drop away; then you will find what was there all along. At the source is the wordless that unites us all."

They shared the meal in silence. Afterwards Hemadri asked them who they were. Savitri glanced quickly and anxiously at Vishnu. Should they tell him that she was a princess, and Vishnu a pancake seller who would one day be king? Or should they just say that they were recently married and following the ancient tradition of seeking the source of the life-giving river before they themselves brought life into the world?

As Vishnu caught Savitri's eye he knew that she, too, was thinking that they should be truthful. The holy man listened without speaking to their story. When they were finished, he said: "As the two of you know that you are equal, one with the other and before the great mystery, so also you already know that you are no different from all others, however humble or lowly their station in life. Seeing the true worth in others will lead you in unexpected directions. Be true to it; it is your guide. Devotion to others is where true awareness leads."

He gestured to show that he had no more to say. They slept the night before the fire, which by morning was just a pile of ash with the barest hint of warmth. Not far from the cave they could hear the sound of the rushing river, tumbling over itself like a playful puppy, but also with the menace of real power.

"Before you set forth on the last stage of your journey," said Hemadri, "you must bathe in the Great River. Go down to the water each in turn, and yield your naked bodies to the purity of the icy water."

First Savitri and then Vishnu did as they were instructed. Using one of the holy man's cooking pots, they each scooped water out of the torrent sweeping by before them. When the water struck their bodies the shock was so great that for a moment they were unable to breathe. And then they took great, deep breaths in rapid succession, sucking in the cold, moist early-morning air until the coldness inside and out was in harmony and every pore of their bodies charged with life.

They said farewell to the wise man. "After you reach the muni's hut, the last part of the journey is a steep climb. To begin with there are some steps carved into the side of the mountain, and then you will find yourself having to pick your way among the mass of boulders left behind by the retreating glacier. There you will find the 'Calf's Mouth' - a cave out of which the river flows at the edge of the glacier. That is the source.

"From there, if you skirt the glacier, you will find a path running round the side of the bare mountain. This is a longer but much gentler descent, which will take you all the way back to the little town of Rikash where you spent the night. Your legs will be very tired and you will find it easier to go down the mountain this way; going down the slippery boulders and the steps in the mountain side can be even harder than climbing up! It means, though, that we will not see each other again; nor will you be passing by the Master again on your way down."

Savitri and Vishnu took leave of the hermit, kneeling before him for his blessing. Once again they made their protesting legs bear them further up the mountain. All day they climbed, sometimes beside the river, which was now much smaller, and sometimes some distance from it.

As evening approached, they saw the hut that the hermit had mentioned. They found that there was an outer room, and then another, inner room. There, sitting silently by the fire, was the Master. He smiled. The fire glowed and occasionally flickered. Great peace filled the room.

Savitri and Vishnu handed their gifts to the Master: the apricots, sultanas and almonds, together with the mangoes. How heavy they had been! They waited expectantly for the Master to bless the food and hand it back to them, or prepare it and share the meal with them. The muni did neither. He simply left the offerings on the floor without paying any attention to them.

They slept the night in the outer room, after cooking some of the other food they had brought. They had taken a bowl to the Master, but he was asleep, the offerings still lying untouched on the floor.

In the morning the Master was nowhere to be seen. Reluctantly, Savitri and Vishnu set off without saying goodbye

as they could not afford to wait. They knew that the last stage would be extremely cold and that they needed to reach the glacier as quickly as possible and to start descending again in good time.

"I just don't understand why he didn't bless and share the food with us," said Savitri as they left. "And now we haven't even been able to say goodbye, as we won't be coming back this way."

The last part of the journey was exactly as Hemadri had told them. The steps up the mountain seemed endless and became more and more slippery the higher they went. Patches of snow began to appear beside the path. The air grew thin.

At last the giant staircase came to an end. They reached a wide, shallow valley. Ahead of them they could see the rough boulders strewn all about, as Hemadri had described. It was then that the weather turned around. In the distance they could see great black clouds forming, which gradually blocked out the sun. The wind sprang up. The two travellers sheltered behind some rocks as a thin curtain of rain and hail swept over them. It was soon past, and the darkness gave way to the brilliance of sunlight dancing in the last remaining raindrops.

They pressed on. After an hour, another squall struck them, but once again did not last long. This time there was some snow.

For the rest of their climb the radiant sunshine would give way to terrifying, swirling darkness, followed again by the return to the intense light. It was as though nature was at war with itself.

Around the middle of the day they came to the glacier and found the Calf's Mouth. Savitri sank to her knees in the hard snow, cupping some of the snow in her hands until it melted and drinking the water. The river was silent now, being no more than a few tiny streams making their way down the mountainside between the boulders. Water seeped out of the ground everywhere. Savitri felt herself part of the great upwelling of life. This was what she had come for. She did not understand it, but she knew its meaning.

Vishnu looked at the grandeur of the mountains, at the clouds sweeping by, at the way in which mere snow and ice had been able to create such a confusion of giant rocks. He marvelled at the power and nobility of his surroundings, feeling at once totally insignificant and utterly in tune with all around him.

Clouds began to sweep over the mountain face. It was snowing, even though it was the wrong time of year. It was time to leave.

They found the other way down with some difficulty. "I don't think we can go down this path," he said to Savitri. "We won't be able to follow it in the snow. The loose pebbles and shale will be wet and slippery and much more dangerous than the steps. At least if we return by the steps they will provide us with little horizontal ledges, no matter how wet they are."

They went back the way they had come. The steep descent tested their legs to the limit. Every now and then they sat down on a step to rest the burning muscles in their legs. Rain, hail and snow continued to sweep across them from time to time. Vishnu grew anxious that they would not reach the muni's hut by nightfall, but made sure that Savitri did not see how worried he was. At last, as they descended further, they emerged from the clouds, and the steps hewn into the cliff face grew drier. They began to make better progress and, just as the last light was fading, found themselves on a gentler path and among trees as they neared the hut.

"We'll surprise him; he won't be expecting to see us again," said Vishnu.

They could see the light of the fire flickering through the doorway. As before the Master was sitting by the fire. He was stirring a small pot and chanting softly, radiating peace.

As they entered the room, he stopped his chanting and bowed his head to them, hands folded. Then the old man reached for three bowls and filled them.

In the bowls was a rich, creamy and smooth dish of rice. And there mixed in were the sultanas, almonds, apricots and mangoes they had brought.

The Boy and The Banana Leaf

Ever since King Raman and the Grand Sultan had set aside their differences by the great river there had been peace between the two lands. As the King grew older, he became less interested in military affairs and, now that the threat to his country had been removed, allowed the army to run down. All that was left was the small Palace Guard.

But the threat had not been removed. Instead, like the wind, it changed direction. To the northeast of the Kingdom of Prithura lay the land of Sinistal: small, rich and peaceable. It was connected to Prithura only by a high pass in the mountains. Just to be on the safe side, King Raman had always had a garrison of soldiers stationed by the pass to prevent any invasion. The soldiers at the pass spent their time playing cards and football as there was little else to do.

One day, however, the Raja of Sinistal died. His younger brother took over as the ruler of the little country. He decided that Sinistal was too small for its many people and, in the dead of night, his army overwhelmed the garrison at the pass with hardly a shot being fired.

The army marched on the city of Prithura. All resistance was swept aside. Word reached the capital before the army arrived and, as they marched along the deeply shaded, mahogany tree-lined avenue towards the Palace, there was not a person to be seen in the streets.

Except, that is, Vishnu the pancake-seller. He continued calmly tending his stall by the Palace gates, clouds of steam rising from the hotplates. The Raja of Sinistal swept up on a magnificent black steed. "Where is the Palace?" he demanded.

Vishnu jerked his thumb over his shoulder.

"Have you no tongue, man?" shouted the Raja. "And take off your cap when you speak to royalty!"

"I will be polite to you when you are polite to me," said Vishnu evenly. "I would gladly welcome you to our town and offer to feed your hungry men, but you have not so much as wished me good day."

"You insolent scoundrel!" roared the Raja. "You will pay for this!"

And the Raja beckoned to his men that they should bind Vishnu hand and foot.

It was still early in the morning. The first low, slanting rays of sunlight cast long shadows behind them.

"I will make an example of this man so that every person in this land will know that I am not to be trifled with!" thundered the Raja so that his words could be heard down the narrow, winding streets of Prithura and inside the very Palace.

Vishnu was dragged into the cobbled town square. There he was to kneel on a rough mat facing the sun until he obeyed the Raja and bowed before him. His shirt was ripped from his body. His hands were untied but his feet remained bound. "Let us see whether your manners have returned when the sun is on the other side of the square," said the Raja, riding off to the edge of the square. Here he dismounted and ordered breakfast for himself and his generals and close advisers. His soldiers stood shoulder to shoulder around the square.

"I know perfectly well who that man is. He can only be Vishnu, the pancake-vendor who married the beautiful Savitri and became king, only to step down as king and become one of the people again. The son of my brother, the late Raja, sought once to win Savitri's hand but she set him an impossible task as a test. He left the country in despair and has never been seen again. I know what power this man has over the people. I will break him.

What a fool I am. Even though the Raja was so off-hand there was no need for me to be rude in return. It was just like when the Grand Sultan of Koh-i-Noor invaded our country. I was civil then, and it took the wind out of his sails. Now I have forgotten my own lesson. Oh, what an idiot I am.

It's hot enough standing here in the shade, and it's still only early morning. I think the Raja will keep him there all day. I don't fancy standing here in the afternoon when the sun swings round but no doubt we soldiers will work in short spells and relieve one another.

These men of mine were an ill-disciplined rabble but I have licked them into shape and now I will show the Raja what we can do. They will stand to attention and not move a muscle all day. Shoulders back, chest out.

It is still only early morning but already this rough mat is beginning to cut into my knees and the sun is burning into my back like a thousand knives. All Prithura will be counting on me, but already I am feeling dizzy.

Fine breakfast. Cowardly lot, the King's soldiers. Nowhere to be seen. Magnificent sight, my men standing motionless to attention in the hot sunlight. Like the look of that sergeant chappie with his fine moustache and his chest all stuck out. Will pin some more ribbons onto that before the day is out.

I am just an onlooker but my heart is thumping. Vishnu is such a hero for us. He had the chance to be king but turned his back on riches and status. He was true to himself and so made it easier for all of us who are poor to accept our lot. And now, there he is, in the middle of the square, in the burning sun, being humiliated. But see how dignified he is! Not moving a muscle.

I have seen other soldiers faint on parade and know that Vishnu cannot last the day. If he does not give in and bow down as he has been commanded he will pass out from exhaustion and topple over. The Raja will take that as the sign he wants.

Looking at these soldiers I can tell that they are wondering whether Vishnu will be able to last the distance. The terrible thing is that if he collapses in the heat the Raja will be triumphant. People are quietly whispering 'He must stay upright, he must stay upright.'

He has been out there for two hours already in the boiling sun. As a soldier he has my respect. I have seen my men collapse on the parade ground. You can discipline them, but there is a limit to what the body can take. This has become a battle. A battle in which the only weapons are the sun and Vishnu's willpower. Shoulders back, chest out.

This confounded man is proving stronger than I had expected. I am getting tired of sitting here and would like to stretch my legs but that would not look good. I cannot move until he gives in. But it is just a matter of time. The sun is nearly at its zenith. Or - is it possible that he could last all day? What would I do then?

Your Highness, I am sure you remember the old story of the sun and the wind and how they looked down and saw a man in a cloak walking along the road. The sun was able to make the man take off his cloak when the wind could not. You will see: Vishnu will never be able to hold out.

Thank you, Grand Vizier. You are right: it is just a matter of time. Order more food and drink!

I don't know if I can last much longer. My knees have gone numb and I can hardly hold myself upright. But I must, for if I fall over the Raja will take it as a victory. Out of the corner of my eye I can see that he himself has not moved from his table since he sat down. He has caught himself in his own trap, for now he knows this he must outlast me or he will be made to look feeble. Somehow I must struggle through to nightfall.

Still our dear Vishnu is not moving! But the heat of the afternoon is only just beginning. Look at the Raja - he is swilling one iced tea after another. And of course he is in the shade and being fanned.

Where has my little boy gone? He has crawled off into the crowd and now I can't see him anywhere. I daren't move; there are soldiers everywhere to make sure the crowd doesn't get out of hand. Oh dear - I do hope and pray he doesn't do something silly, for I can see these soldiers will stop at nothing.

This is extremely embarrassing. I can see a small boy crawling through people's legs. Everyone else is standing stock still as they should, but with their former King still holding out so against the heat of the sun it would look really bad if I ordered my soldiers to punish the boy. Perhaps he will just find his way back to his mother. Shoulders back now, head up and show them your fine moustache.

I cannot believe this - a little boy has just emerged from the ranks of the spectators and is running over to Vishnu. My sergeant has gone puce in the face and is looking towards the Raja for instructions, but the Raja will not catch his eye. People are beginning to laugh. The boy has reached Vishnu! Now he is standing there holding a banana leaf over his head, just like soldiers are shading the Raja with their palm leaves.

That sergeant who was sticking out his chest is trying to catch my eye but I cannot be seen to give an instruction for the boy to be punished. Come, man, do your duty!

The Raja will not look my way. He cannot be seen to be giving the order. That wretched boy is providing Vishnu with shade. This will never do. I will have to act.

The sergeant is marching out into the square! The people around me are beginning to hiss and boo. He has scooped the little boy up under his arm and now he has dumped him back with his mother. He is making an announcement! He bellows like a bull, this man. The next person who so much as moves will be shot, he roars.

My prayers have been heard! My boy has come back to me unhurt! I shall hold on to him tightly, but what a wriggler he is. It is so difficult to explain to him that he must stay quiet. He is such a spirited little chap and never listens.

That little boy has given me hope. He is not afraid of the soldiers or the Raja. He even made the crowd laugh for a moment. But I must forget about everything that is happening around me and draw strength from the silence of the crowd. I feel myself being drawn into the future. The road, the castle at the end and myself are all becoming one.

I cannot believe this. The little boy has escaped again and is once again moving out towards Vishnu with his banana leaf. What will the sergeant do? I see him raising his rifle to his shoulder - but look! The Raja has lifted his finger.

My boy! My boy! He will be shot - no, the sergeant has lowered his gun again. I think the Raja may have given some kind of sign. I cannot believe that my restless, spirited little boy is standing there so quietly, like a soldier to attention. Why, he is as still as Vishnu himself.

This is a bad business, very bad business. It is not reflecting well on my master. But, it's an ill wind that blows nobody any good: if the Raja is humiliated, I am next in line, and so will become ruler of Sinistal without even needing to plot or fight against the Raja, who is really a very stupid man. 'Ah, yes, Your Highness, it is very wise of you to have instructed the sergeant to lower his rifle. That would have made us look very bad. At a stroke you have shown your future subjects what a great and gracious ruler you are, deeply esteemed Raja.' Hah! He looks better. I think he liked the sound of that.

What a poltroon this Grand Vizier of mine is. So fawning and full of flattery. I see through him and don't trust him an inch. In fact, when this is over I will sack him, together with that idiot of a sergeant. My goodness, the heat beating off the cobblestones is insufferable. My clothes are drenched with sweat. My bottom is sticking to the seat. I need to stretch my legs. This is unbearable. And still it is only early afternoon. But even with that boy holding the banana leaf over his head, Vishnu looks very weak and wobbly.

This Vishnu is quite a man. I can't think of any of our soldiers - not even the toughest in my regiment - who could have held out for as long like this. He has my respect. He is a true soldier. I would follow him to the ends of the earth.

Onlookers in the sun are beginning to faint. It is a miracle that Vishnu is still there, kneeling in exactly the same position. Oh, as a citizen of Prithura how my heart swells with pride: he is worth a hundred armies!

Now what has happened? That wretched little boy has fainted in the sun. No one is moving. They are just leaving him there. Why doesn't that fool of a sergeant drag him off the square? I can't catch his eye.

This little boy has made a fool of me twice. I won't be made a fool of a third time. He can just lie there in the sun. If the Raja wants me to do anything about it, he can issue a proper order.

Look! Vishnu has reached out with one hand and pulled the banana leaf over the little boy to shade him. Now his arm is by his side again and he is kneeling just as before.

I am still on the road and can see the castle. I am the road, and am in the castle. I am at peace. There is a rustling beside me. I see my arm going out and doing something with - I'm not sure what it is, it doesn't matter, I am just here, have always been here and will always be here. My mind and my body and my spirit all rolled into one.

The sun is getting lower. Shadows are stretching out from the trees. More of us are in the shade now and the worst sting has gone out of the sun's rays.

I am getting so stiff that I will hardly be able to get up by myself. It is getting cooler but I am still bathed in sweat and it is taking all my willpower to remain in my seat. What a leader I am, that I have been able to sit here for most of the day without stirring even though I feel so uncomfortable. The food these soldiers are preparing for me is terrible. I just want to change my clothes, have a long cool bath and then recline in splendour in the King's palace. It won't be long now: Prince Vishnu cannot possibly last the day.

This is unbelievable. We soldiers have not been relieved and have been forced to stand here all day, in the sun and now in the shade as the sun drops below the buildings. It will not be long now before the sun has set. If Vishnu lasts until then - well, I cannot even begin to imagine what will happen.

I truly think that Vishnu is going to last until sundown. His body is as still as a statue. He looks as though he is far away in spirit and totally at peace. The rays of the sun are becoming fainter; in minutes the sun will have set.

A tremor went through the crowd as the last tiny golden sliver of the sun slipped behind the horizon. No one moved. The Raja looked on in horror. The Grand Vizier looked pale, but a little smile played around the corners of his mouth. Some of the spectators who had fainted in the heat began to stir; it was the only motion in the crowd. None of the soldiers dared move. The sergeant looked steadily at the ground.

As though the wind was lifting its corners, the banana leaf began to stir. Hands and then a head appeared from under the leaf. The boy peered around in confusion. He looked out, and saw that the sun had set. Unsteadily, he got to his feet.

Putting his hands under Vishnu's shoulders, the boy pulled him up with all his might. It was almost possible to hear Vishnu's stiffened muscles as they came out of their locked positions. At length, Vishnu got back up on his feet. He looked steadily towards the Raja, and then - bowed.

The Raja did not know where to look. The sergeant turned round and began to walk away. The soldiers drifted off, heading down the road back to their own country in twos and threes. The Grand Vizier fainted. The boy's mother ran out into the square and scooped him up. People ran to the palace and unlocked the guardroom, where the royal guard - the only soldiers in Prithura - had been locked up. The king and queen were released from their chambers.

Stallholders began to light the oil-lamps on their little carts. Steam began to rise from the hotplates of the pancake stall.

Chess in the Afternoon

Gopal and Chandra were playing their usual afternoon game of chess in the main square of Prithura. They were sitting at a table under a leafy tree outside a café. They were both elderly, and they were both wealthy.

Their games generally ended either when they became very excited or when they grew bored. Today they were bored. The game had fizzled out in a draw and they watched the world go by as they sipped at their long, iced mango drinks.

"How is that daughter of yours doing, Gopal?" asked Chandra.

"Lakshmi? Why, she is still working in a bank in Calcutta," replied Gopal. "Doing very well and making lots of money."

"That's all banks do, steal people's money," grumbled Chandra, hoping to provoke Gopal. But the sun was shining, the birds were singing and his business was doing well. He did not feel like quarrelling with his friend today. Yesterday Chandra had thrown the board up in the air when he had lost, scattering pieces all over the pavement. Gopal still smiled inwardly thinking back on the event. That was one of his most satisfying wins ever. As usual there had been a little gaggle of urchins watching the game, hoping for some excitement.

"As long as it goes into my daughter's pocket, that's all right by me," said Gopal.

"The rich stealing from the poor, if you ask me," said Chandra.

"No one is asking you," said Gopal pointedly.

Got him, thought Gopal. As good as a brilliant chess move. It was a pity the game was over, or the board might have gone up in the air again.

"At least it makes a change from the poor stealing from the rich, as happens here all the time," said Chandra. "Can't trust them an inch."

Now Gopal gave a lot of money to charity and was a great champion of the poor. He had even had an orphanage named after him. Pretty sharp move, thought Chandra to himself, knowing how Gopal hated any criticism of the poor. That will stop him being so smug.

Gopal went red in the face and was just about to slam his fists on the table and make the chess pieces dance, but the birds were still singing and the sun was still shining and he decided not to let his friend get the better of him.

"My dear Chandra, sometimes you say things just like you play chess, without any thought at all. Everyone knows that the poor are much more honest than the rich."

"Ooooh, are they?" said Chandra rolling his eyes. "That's news to me. What about the other day, when you left your hat behind and it was gone when we returned two minutes later?"

"I expect someone picked it up by mistake."

"Which is why it was on sale in the market the next day, I suppose?" inquired Chandra politely.

"It wasn't the same hat!" snapped Gopal. "It had a different colour hatband."

"That's only because yours was so dirty. You could tell it was your hat from the dent in the side when you jumped on it after losing that game."

I'm in good form, thought Chandra. If this were chess it would be nearly checkmate. How's he going to wriggle out of this one? Some of the urchins were laughing. That always infuriated Gopal.

But not this time. Gopal knew what Chandra was up to and decided to play him at his own game.

"For a rich person you are certainly generous with your money the way you throw it away." Chandra was a notorious gambler. He would gamble on anything - horses, dogs, tomorrow's weather, which cockroach would be first to reach some food. "Let us have a little bet to see who is right."

"What sort of bet?" said Chandra, sitting up straight.

"Well," said Gopal, "what say we get one of these boys here to drop a 100 rupee note by the fountain. I say that poor people will try to return it to its rightful owner, while rich people will quietly pocket it. If I am right, you will put up the next 100 rupee bill and pay me 100 rupees, while if you are right I will put up the next stake and pay you 100 rupees."

"I see," said Chandra. "So if the person who picks it up is poor and keeps it, I win, but if the person is rich and keeps it, you win. And the other way round. I can see that I am going to make a lot of money this afternoon, dear Gopal!"

"No, what you will see is that the rich are grasping, but the poor are generous."

"Right!" said Chandra, getting into the spirit of things with no difficulty at all. "First time round we split the stake, then." And he produced a 50 rupee note from his wallet. Gopal pulled a 100 rupee note out of his pocket and took the 50 rupee note. "Now we are in for 50 rupees each. Here, Chapal," he said, beckoning to a particularly scruffy urchin, "take this note over to the fountain, drop it on the ground when no one is looking and then walk away."

Chapal took the note and ran across to the fountain. Chandra and Gopal strained forward to see what was happening. Chapal dropped the note on the ground, looked round quickly, picked it up again and made off with it as though a hundred hyenas were on his tail.

Chandra roared with laughter. "First game to me!" he said. "What a sly rascal."

Gopal was going red in the face, but just managed to control himself. He took two further 100 rupee notes out of his pocket, giving one to Chandra and one to a small girl. "Now, Nandita," he said, "you go and do the same, except you must promise not to run off with the note."

"Perhaps you should pay her to be honest," said Chandra, shaking with laughter. "Give her a bribe to make sure she doesn't trick you."

"I won't trick you," said Nandita proudly. And she walked quickly over to the fountain, dropped the note when nobody was looking, and returned to where Chandra and Gopal were sitting.

For a long time nobody noticed the note at all. At last a mangy looking dog came by, sniffed at the note and then picked it up in its mouth and ran off with it.

"Hey!" shouted Chandra, springing to his feet and running after the dog. "Stop thief!"

The dog ran off gaily, its head in the air, darting this way and that. It was enjoying the chase. Suddenly it came to an abrupt halt when Uttam the rope seller slung a length of rope around his neck. The dog tumbled over and Uttam retrieved the note. "Is this yours, Sir?" he said, holding it out to Chandra.

Chandra reluctantly took the note and walked slowly back to the table. This time it was Gopal who was convulsed with laughter. "You should simply have let the dog go," he said. "Definitely a poor dog. You would have won another 100 rupees."

Chandra glared at him. From his wallet he took out the 100 rupee note that Gopal had given him moments before, and passed the banknote - now slightly moist - that had been rescued from the dog to one of the other children.

Once again it took some time before someone spotted the money. This time it was an extremely rich, fat lady. Both Chandra and Gopal recognised her. "Oh, Padmini!" exclaimed Chandra. "She has so much money it is a wonder she is not dropping banknotes herself. You will see, she has no need of more and will give it to the first deserving person she sees."

That person turned out to be Padmini herself. Swooping down with a grace and ease unlikely in one so large, she scooped up the banknote and calmly tucked it away in her ample bosom. Gopal banged the table in delight. The chess pieces jiggled up and down, the children shrieked with laughter, and Padmini looked around in some astonishment. She came over to the table. "It's my lucky day," she said, extracting the banknote from her bosom. "Look what I have just found," she said innocently. "Here, Gopal, give this to your orphanage. I know it always needs money." And she strode off, looking slightly less red in the face.

"There you are," said Chandra, "honest as the day is long."

"You're not fooling me," said Gopal. "What do you think, children, would she have given it to us if we hadn't all been making such a noise?"

"No!!" they all shouted. Some adults, who were beginning to take an interest in the proceedings, joined in too. Chandra decided there was no point trying to bluff any further and slapped two more 100 rupee bills on the table.

Once again Nandita took one and ran over to the fountain. This time she dropped it not on the cobblestones but on the edge of the fountain. She ran back to the ever-growing group of people.

The wind caught the banknote and deposited it in the water. Chandra was about to get to his feet and dash over to fish it out before it sank when a small boy espied the note, drifting on the water. The boy was grubby and dressed in ragged clothes. As he leant over to grab the banknote a gust of wind suddenly sent it scurrying across the surface of the water like a small sailing boat. The boy stretched out further and further and, just as his hand closed around the banknote, fell into the pond.

He came up choking and spluttering and it was clear he couldn't swim. Displaying an admirable turn of speed, Chandra got to the fountain first and hauled the boy out. He held him upside down until no more water was running out and then set him back on his feet.

"A draw, I think," said Gopal. "We have no way of knowing what he would have done with the money. Since our little experiment nearly killed him, I suggest we let him keep the money."

Chandra agreed. He did not want to appear mean. They went back to their table. Once again a 100 rupee note was produced. Another small boy took it over to the fountain. He placed it on the edge, as Nandita had done, but this time put a small stone on top of it to stop it blowing away. He rejoined the spectators.

This time it was a holy man who spotted the banknote. He had come to pray at the fountain, which was something of a shrine. There to his surprise were more riches than would come his way in an entire year. This must surely be a gift from on high, he decided. He held the note up against the light to check that it was genuine and then stuffed it into his loincloth. He sat down in front of the fountain in the lotus position and closed his eyes.

Chandra and Gopal ran over to him. "I've won," Chandra shouted on the way. "A poor man has kept the banknote!" "Nonsense!" puffed Gopal. "He's a holy man. He means to share it with the poor."

The astonished yogi found himself being violently shaken in the midst of his meditations. "What are you going to do with that money?" two old, overweight and wealthy gentleman were shouting at him in unison.

The yogi decided that the only thing to do was to resume his worship. He closed his eyes. Chandra and Gopal felt abashed that they had interfered with his daily devotions. They slunk back to the table.

"Shall we play chess?" one of them said.

Dark Durga

Samir ran a basket stall, not far from the Palace gates. He spread his baskets out in a little area set aside for a shrine to the many-armed goddess Durga. People would come and pray at the shrine or to light a candle, so it was good for business. There might not be much connection between baskets and this goddess riding on a tiger, but her many arms provided a convenient display stand for Samir's woven baskets. No-one seemed to mind. Both the goddess and the tiger were entirely black, either from all the dirt and grime they had gathered over the years or because they were made that way. Nobody knew. The statue was simply known as Dark Durga.

People would sometimes leave offerings of food, wrapped in bamboo leaves, at the foot of the little statue, which stood on a stone column. Samir acted as unofficial priest to the shrine and, towards the end of the day, would quietly retrieve all the food parcels from the top of the column. In the morning, the passers-by would note to their satisfaction that Durga and the tiger had eaten up all the food during the night. Of course, they knew that it had really been taken away by Samir but did not think about it too much as they liked to believe that miraculous things were happening in their little grotto set into the Palace hillside.

One evening, just as Samir was packing away his things and scooping up the little food parcels into one of his rush baskets, a little voice said, "Why are you taking away their food?"

Samir spun round to see a little girl with big brown eyes. Hastily he brushed the ledge around the bottom of the statue and put the food back. "I am not taking away the food," he said, "but have to make sure that it is all kept nice and clean. And what is your name?"

"Kalika," she replied.

"Kalika," said Samir, "that's a pretty name. Now Kalika, if you come back first thing in the morning you will see that all the food has gone."

"But you'll just take it again as soon as I turn my back," she said.

Samir was not quite sure what to do. He could see that she

really wanted to believe that Durga and her tiger ate up all the food at night. If the adults believed that this was what happened even though they knew otherwise, he decided that he should arrange things so that little Kalika would think that way too.

"We'll both leave together," he said. "That way you can be sure the food has been left behind."

"Someone else will take it," she objected.

Samir could see that he had run into someone with an unfortunately logical turn of mind. It was all the more important for her to find some magic in her life.

As it happened, the shrine was set into the rock face of the hill. Once upon a time, Durga had been strictly worshipped by royalty and the nobles alone - which is why the shrine was so close to the Palace. At that time, there had been an official Keeper of the Shrine and, when the Keeper went home at night, some folding iron gates were pulled across and locked. No one could get in.

For many years now, the shrine had become a popular one that was open to the general public, and the gates were never used. Samir was not even sure they would still work but, hoping that the gods were on his side, tugged at them and, after clearing away some creeper that had wound itself through them, was pleased to find that they pulled shut. He wound a stout rope through the gates and made a firm knot.

"Someone could undo the knot," said the logical girl.

With just a touch of weariness, Samir undid the rope and rummaged in his possessions, looking for a padlock he knew he had somewhere. By now there was a small crowd of people looking on with interest. They wanted their shrine to be a good shrine from which the food disappeared every night, but they also enjoyed watching Samir's struggle with the little girl.

At last, the shrine was firmly locked up, with the food neatly in place on the ledge.

"You could just come back later and undo the lock," she went on. "How can I know you won't trick me?"

"Because," said an old man with a long white beard called Trilochan, "I always sleep here, near the shrine, and have enormous ears like an elephant, so that I can hear everything. I can even wiggle them about," he declared. And with that he did

indeed make his ears move backwards and forwards and jiggle about in a way that made all the children in the little crowd shriek with a mixture of laughter and fear.

Kalika was persuaded. But Samir was not. Once home, he said to his wife, Lakshmi: "You will see, that girl is like a mongoose, she will not let go. She will be there first thing in the morning before I open up and the food will still be there."

"Of course it won't," said Lakshmi calmly, "the mice will get it."

"The pedestal is too smooth for mice to get up," said Samir.

"Well, rats then."

"I have seen them try during the day and they can't get up it either," declared Samir.

"Oh well, birds then," said Lakshmi brightly.

Samir observed that there were no birds at night.

There was also not much sleep for him that night. It was all very well for people to turn a blind eye to the fact that he took the food parcels but, now that he had been challenged, it was essential for them to be gone by morning or he would be made to look a rogue. As unofficial keeper of the Shrine he would become a laughing stock and people would stop buying his baskets. His blood ran hot and cold.

The next morning, Samir went as usual to the shrine at the crack of dawn. Kalika was already there. "The food is gone!" she said excitedly, jumping up and down. "Dark Durga and her tiger have eaten it!"

Samir was mightily relieved and put up with some good-natured leg pulling for the rest of the day from the other stallholders: Uttam the rope seller, Kanak the carpet seller and Neelam, with her little mountains of purple, yellow, emerald, ochre and indigo incense powders.

At the end of the day, he was just about to scoop up the rather larger than usual quantity of bamboo leaf food parcels that had been left during the day, when a small voice behind him said:

"I'm watching you."

Samir hastily went into cleaning mode again, put back the parcels and locked the shrine up as he had the night before. He and Kalika walked back home together until their paths diverged shortly before Samir's shanty dwelling.

Lakshmi thought it was very funny that Kalika was still keeping an eye on him but was less amused that Samir had not brought home the normal family dinner in the form of the food offerings. She had to borrow and beg from neighbours, as she had very little in the house with which to cook.

Day after day went by until Kalika became tired of checking whether the food was gone. But instead of Kalika all sorts of other people now came to check up that the miracle was happening every night. Samir was not sure how it was happening but just smiled a little knowing smile and quietly gave thanks each day to Dark Durga. Perhaps there was a particularly agile high-jumper rat among the Shrine pack. But what if this super athlete got fat on his newfound diet and was no longer able to leap as high as the ledge? Samir looked at his stocks of unsold baskets and shuddered.

Samir decided that he had to know how the food was being removed. Lakshmi interrupted her basket-making and looked up at him with wide eyes when he said that he would hide nearby one night and wait until he saw who took the food.

"You, the keeper of the shrine," she said. "Shame on you! All these years Durga has been good enough to let you take the food and now that she is taking it herself, you, of all people, don't believe the legend. You're worse than that Kalika. If people find out that you do not even believe they will stop coming to the shrine and buying the baskets."

She was right. Sales had been just amazing since the story of the food had got about. So Samir decided to have a quiet word with Trilochan, the man with the long white beard.

"Trilochan," he said, "does not your name mean the one with three eyes?"

"It does indeed," the old man said.

"Well, I was wondering whether one night you could keep your third eye open and tell me what happens to the food that is left out every night."

"But you know what happens to the food," said Trilochan with a twinkle in his eye, or perhaps all three eyes, "Durga ..."

"Yes," said Samir impatiently, "but I have to be sure."

Trilochan remained silent. As it happened Trilochan

already knew what was happening to the food. He had been intrigued himself for some time and, indeed, had wondered whether it might be possible to make some kind of fishing rod with which he could "catch" some of the food parcels - as he got quite hungry, too. But instead he discovered that the culprit was Bobo, the big fat grey monkey from the Palace gardens. In the early hours of the morning, Bobo would make his way soundlessly to the shrine, where he was able to climb down and back up again from an overhanging tree. Bobo had to be very careful, as people hated monkeys coming into the town, so he acted very stealthily, and only Trilochom ever saw him.

One day, Bobo died. Fortunately, the food parcels keep disappearing. Then, some time later, Trilochan himself lay dying. Samir came to visit him. "I have a confession to make, Samir," said Trilochan. "All those years, it was Bobo who took the food offerings."

"But Bobo's dead," said Samir, "and still the parcels are disappearing. So how is that happening?"

Trilochan rolled his eyes and was about to tell Samir when he breathed his last. As Samir gathered up Trilochan's pitiful little collection of possessions, he came across the fishing line and hook. He understood. Far from stealing, Trilochan had simply taken over public-spiritedly from Bobo to keep the Shrine tradition alive.

Now it was up to him, Samir. He decided that the only thing would be to open up the shrine very early the next morning, and remove the food parcels before anyone came along. They would be a little stale, but perhaps still good enough for that evening's supper. Lakshmi would be pleased.

Samir got there while it was still dark and the sun no more than a hint of pink peeping through the tall stands of bamboo. He was about to open up when he noticed that someone was there before him.

It was Kalika. She was now a fine young woman, who went to university, where she studied modern religion.

"You are very early today, Samir," she smiled. Samir looked uncomfortable. However would he remove the food now?

But then, to his inexpressible relief, he saw that the food was gone.

Catching the look in his eye, Kalika said, "Oh that you should have so little faith in your own Durga, Samir! Surely by now, after all these years, you too realise that it is she who takes the food?"

For the next few mornings, Samir would find Kalika already there when he came to open up. Perhaps as part of her religious studies, Kalika had decided it was important for the disappearing food tradition to be kept going. First it had been Bobo, then Trilochan, now Kalika. He felt his heart lifting as he realised that the Dark Durga would always find a way.

Then early one morning, just as he was leaving for the shrine, he found a note pinned to his door. It was from Kalika. "I am ill and can't meet you at the shrine," it said. Samir smiled to himself. He was right: it had been Kalika who was removing the offerings, and now she had sent her little brother with a message of warning so that he could make sure the goddess's wishes were carried out. How strange: just when he had almost reached the point at which he believed the legend himself.

So Samir hastened off to the Shrine. He didn't bother to have breakfast, as he knew there would be plenty of food parcels to dispose of.

He reached the Shrine as the first of the sunlight poked its pink fingers through the black bamboo. He hung his cloak up on a tree and went over to unlock the gates.

The ledge was empty.

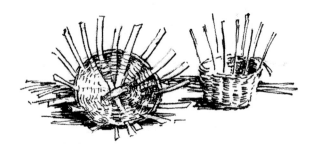

The Urban Hermit

No one knew where he had come from. All at once he had become a fixture in the main square. Some said that he was a hermit who had come from one of the caves near the Great River. Others said that he was a holy man who had left an *ashram*, where yogis live. Others again said that he was an escaped criminal.

Whoever he was, it was impossible to find out, as he didn't speak. He just slept in the square, did some stretching exercises and walked about in small circles and spent a lot of time in the lotus position or standing on his head. People would leave him food, just in case he was a holy man. His ribs stuck out pitifully above his loincloth. With his bushy black beard there was also something slightly sinister about him, so it wasn't a bad idea to get on side, just in case.

When people left food that needed to be cooked he would gather up sticks from under the trees or break up a palm frond that had come down and make a little fire. Sometimes, when he was feeling particularly adventurous, he would make his way over to Vishna's pancake stall, where he could usually be sure of receiving some leftovers.

One day, to everyone's amazement, he was found lying on an old, rusty iron bed with sagging springs. Where he had found it during the night no one knew. He tied some loose plastic sheeting over the bed frame and, when it rained, transferred downstairs, lying on a roll-up sleeping mat - his only other possession.

Children would go up to him and ask him his name. He would stay silent. They would ask him where he had come from and how long he was staying, but he wouldn't reply. Sometimes the children would even say very rude things to him, but nothing would provoke him to speak. He would not even look people in the eye. Some people asked how you could be a hermit in a town; but others said that there was nothing lonelier than to be alone in a crowd, which showed he was a true yogi.

Eventually, even the children stopped trying to taunt him and get him to speak. He became part of the local scene. They called him the Urban Hermit. More and more people began to bring him food. His fame began to spread beyond the town of Prithura.

Over at Dark Durga's shrine, however, all was not well. "People used to leave food at the shrine. Now they leave it with that wretched fake hermit," grumbled Neelam, weighing out some coloured powders, "and we don't get any. Not that we ever used to take it," she added hastily.

"Things haven't been the same since Trilocham died," said Uttam the rope seller. "He used to keep a watchful eye on the shrine at night to make sure that no one stole the food from Dark Durga. Every morning the food would be gone. Now there are not even any offerings when Samir opens up the shine in the morning, or when he leaves at night. Meanwhile, that hermit just grows fatter."

"We will have to do something," said Kanak the carpet seller. "I would be happy to stay awake all night, like Trilocham used to do, but if there is no food to guard what's the use?"

Samir's wife Lakshmi was also becoming upset at the lack of food offerings that Samir was able to smuggle home. One day the five of them sat down on one of Kanak's carpets to discuss what to do.

"Durga is displeased," said Samir. "She is punishing us because she is no longer given food by the people. My business has collapsed because people aren't coming to check the miracle of how the goddess and her tiger are taking the food at night."

"If we could persuade that hermit to move over here," said

Uttam slowly, "then people would bring their food to the shrine and all would be well again."

There was a stunned silence. It was agreed that this was a brilliant idea. Without further ado, Neelam, Uttam, Samir, Lakshmi and Kanak made their way to the square and approached the hermit. Samir introduced himself as the keeper of the shrine to Dark Durga.

"The goddess is angry because the people are no longer giving her food. She asks that you move your bed to the shrine."

The hermit did not move, did not speak, and did not look them in the eye. He just rolled over and closed his eyes. Lakshmi pleaded, Neelam scolded, Uttam roared at him, Kanak poked him in the ribs and Samir tried to reason. It was no use.

"Shame on you," said Padmini the rich woman, "for pestering a poor and innocent man. No wonder Durga is punishing you. Now I really am convinced he is a holy man."

Durga's five devotees returned to Kanak's carpet to confer. Evening fell. Oil lamps and braziers were lit. Everywhere groups of people were eating and chatting. One by one the lights and fires were extinguished. Then, in the very dead of night, when dreams are at their deepest and all is silent, the hermit had a wonderful sensation that he was being rocked gently on a flying carpet.

When the birds began singing and he woke up, he found to his astonishment that his bed was now stationed beside the shrine to Dark Durga. Samir the shrine-keeper arrived and unlocked the gates. People began arriving and placing food parcels on the ledge in the shrine as they used to.

"I wondered where the hermit had gone!" said Ramita, a toothless old lady who had found that her aching back was much better ever since she had been leaving food for the hermit. "Luckily I saw the sign saying that he had moved to the shrine. This is even better. Now I can leave the food with Dark Durga, to be blessed by her first before the hermit partakes of it."

But the hermit did not do much partaking. As before, Samir would close the shrine gates at night, the ledges bulging with little food parcels. In the morning, the food would all be gone. Samir's basket business boomed again, Uttam was selling lots of rope, Kanak's carpets were flying out of his little shop and Neelam was constantly weighing out coloured powders. Lakshmi, too, looked happy.

Several nights later, when the hermit was feeling extremely hungry, he woke up in the early hours. On the other side of the gates, the shrine was groaning with food. Surely the goddess would not mind if he shared some of it. But the gates were locked. When he began rattling them, Uttam, his black beard even larger than the hermit's own, suddenly appeared menacingly before him. The hermit shrank back onto his creaking, rusty bed.

The next morning Samir and the others discovered that the hermit had somehow picked up his bed during the night and returned to the square. "I can't believe it," said Kanak. "That bed weighs a ton. Well, of course, it *looks* as though it does; I haven't ever actually lifted it!"

The next night the hermit once again had the sensation of rocking gently on a magic carpet. He was about to shout out and protest, when he remembered that he couldn't speak. In no time at all he found himself right beside the shrine again. With Uttam looking down at him in a particularly threatening way, the holy man rolled over and went to sleep.

In the morning, the hermit got up and began tugging at his bed in order to take it back to the square. The bed would not budge. The harder he tugged, the more firmly stuck it seemed to be. He looked down and saw that ropes had been attached to the four legs and fastened to rings in the ground to which donkeys and other animals were generally tethered during the day. The more he pulled at the knots, the tighter they became. His poor, thin fingers were no match for the knots, which had evidently been tied by an expert. Uttam was whistling in the background.

All day, the hermit lay lying on his bed, quietly studying the construction of the gates to the shrine. That night, wracked with hunger, he woke up in the early hours. Stealthily, he moved over to the gates, placing his foot on one of the decorative scrolls, from where he was sure he would be able to hoist his other leg up over the top of the gate. But just as he did so, he became aware of a ghostly figure with a kind of fishing rod. By his side was a bucket, already full of little food parcels.

"Hey!" shouted the hermit. "You're stealing from the shrine!" The hermit caught sight of a beard, even blacker than the night, swirling around as the figure looked up. "Thief! Durga burglar!" he roared.

People began to wake up. "The hermit can speak, the hermit can speak!" they shouted excitedly. "Imposter! Fraud! Cheat!"

For a moment the hermit was rooted to the spot. He went red and then white in the face. Then, pausing only to scoop up the bucket full of food offerings, he made off at high speed into the night. He was never seen again.

After the knots had been untied, the iron bedstead was carried by a group of ghostly figures down to the river, and was also never seen again.

The Second Urban Hermit

"Another one's arrived," said Uttam the ropemaker.

"Another what?" said Samir, glancing up from the basket he was weaving.

"Another of those hermits. Over there, in the square," replied Uttam, jerking his thumb over his shoulder.

"What, like that one who brought his bed?"

"Yes, except that this one at least just has a mat which he rolls out. Why do these fellows keep popping up? It's like some kind of disease."

"Well, we got rid of the last one quickly enough," said Kanak brightly, unrolling one of his carpets.

"But I didn't like the way we did it," said Neelam, measuring out some of her purple, orange and green powders. "We were very hard on him."

"He was a fraud," protested Uttam, swinging a length of rope around his head. "Pretended he couldn't speak when he could. We'll get this one too."

"I think Neelam is right," said Jagadeep the fishmonger. "It was just because people started giving him the food they normally leave at our shrine, that's what upset us."

"Our business suffered," said Kanak firmly. "We can't have that. It's hard enough surviving as it is."

"What I don't understand," said Samir, "is how you can be a hermit in a town. If you want to be a hermit, you go off and find a cave or some lonely place. But why take up position in the middle of the town and then pretend no one is there?"

"I think we should ask him," said Neelam. "What's more, we could invite him to come over here to the shrine, like we did the last one. If he's a good yogi, people would flock to see him and our business would flourish."

"He'll probably be another one of those who doesn't speak," said Uttam gloomily. "Or he'll be too busy standing on his head to talk to us."

"What we would have to do is share the food offerings decently with him," said Samir.

"Whatever are you saying, Samir?" demanded Kanak,

displaying one of his carpets on top of Uttam's coils of rope. "You know that it is Durga who takes the food. That is the miracle of the shrine."

A number of people were standing around now, listening to the discussion among the street traders.

"Oh, yes, of course," said Samir hastily. "I meant that – that we could encourage some of the people bringing food to the shine to give some to the holy man too, if that is what he is."

"I don't mind so long as it's good for business," said Uttam, "but if you ask me these hermits and yogis are all phoneys and cheats."

"You might find that this one could do the Indian rope trick with some of your rope," said Neelam. "Now that really would bring in business."

It would also, Uttam reflected to himself, be a good way to scale the fence when the shrine was locked up at night. Kanak had been practising for years to get one of his carpets to fly, but had never succeeded. It wasn't just the food offerings that people left behind; apart from his fishing rod, which he used to hook up the little food parcels in the small hours of the night, Uttam also had a long bamboo pole with a small brush on one end. This he would use to scoop the coins people had left behind into a little tin on the end of another piece of bamboo. But he would have to take this fellow into his confidence, as he would be bound to see what Uttam got up to at night.

"All right," said Uttam, reluctantly. " Let's go and talk to him."

So they all made their way over to the town square where, sure enough, another hermit had taken up station. "You men are all much too aggressive," said Neelam. "Leave the talking to me."

The yogi was standing on his head. "Been doing that for the last four hours, he has," said a bystander.

Neelam bent down until her head was upside down too and looked the hermit in the eye. "Do you

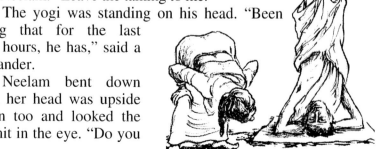

mind if I ask you a few questions?" she said.

"Not at all," said the yogi, swinging his legs down gracefully and standing up. "I always like it when people speak to me."

A murmur of approval went through the knot of onlookers.

"The thing is," said Neelam, "that we don't understand how you can be a hermit in the midst of all this hustle and bustle."

"Ah, but that's the whole point," said the man in the simple white garment. "I lived in a cave for many years. I got used to the silence. It felt comfortable. I hardly ever saw anyone. I realised that I had taken the aloneness as far as I could. Here, in the town, I have to learn to be alone in a crowd. That is much, much harder."

"But you are hardly alone if you start chatting to people," said Neelam. "Then you are just like anyone else, except that you do unusual things like standing on your head."

"Can you do the Indian rope trick, by any chance?" came a voice from the crowd.

"*Be quiet*, Uttam," said Neelam crossly. "Please - what does it mean, to be a hermit in a town?"

"It means," said the man, "learning to live in my own world without being distracted by anything around me. I am happy to talk to people now as it is better for you to know what I am doing. Once you are used to me, you will leave me alone. Then you will know that if I don't reply I am not being rude, but that it is part of my journey. I am a seeker of God."

"Samir here is the keeper of the shine to Dark Durga," Neelam said, seizing the opportunity. "He was wondering whether you might be happier near our shrine."

"I don't see why not," said the stranger. "Let me just get my things."

He picked up his bedroll. "Off we go."

And so it was that the hermit made his new home near the shrine. "At least he doesn't have a long black beard like that other fellow," said Uttam.

"But Uttam, you have a long black beard," observed Kanak drily.

"Mine is flowing and magnificent," he said stroking his beard lovingly. "His was ragged and dirty."

Even though he was disappointed to discover that the

hermit did not know the Indian rope trick, Uttam treated him politely and gave him the benefit of the doubt.

As the hermit had said, once people knew what he was doing, they left him alone to get on with it. He receded into the background and for a while hardly anyone noticed him any more. People left him food offerings and, to begin with, Uttam made sure that the hermit shared in the nightly raids on the food that had been left behind in the shrine.

The hermit did not say anything when he saw Uttam each night put out his strange contraptions to extract the offerings from the shrine. Instead, he simply took up residence in the shrine itself. This suited everyone. It meant the shrine was guarded and that Samir no longer had to open up first thing in the morning. Uttam could now get a full night's sleep. And as before, the food that had been presented to the goddess during the day had miraculously disappeared by morning. Nobody asked too many questions.

Except for Samir. He was intrigued by the hermit. Although the hermit increasingly wanted to be left alone, he found himself engaged in long conversations with Samir.

"Why is it so important for you to be alone in the midst of all the busyness?" Samir would ask.

"Because that way I can find the stillness within. It is easy to be still in a cave all by yourself. But when I am surrounded by all the people scurrying to and fro and by the buffalo and cows and goats in the street, and when traders are shouting out their wares and haggling, and when the scents of a thousand and one oils and spices are in my nostrils, then I must retreat fully into the silence of my inner world."

"But what good is that to you? Why not just be part of the world?"

"Because I can only truly be part of the world if I can go wholly within. That is my task. I want to be as close to the source of all things as I can."

"Why not let the source of all things be close to you?"

The hermit did not have an answer. In fact, he did not like Samir's questions, and gradually they too ceased speaking. He was considered very devout and his fame began to spread. People would come to consult him. "Will I have another child, oh Nameless One?" asked a large woman with eight children. "If you don't speak, I will know it is meant to be."

The yogi was silent. Some months later the woman came back triumphantly with a baby in her arms. "The Nameless One was right! He knew the will of God!" she proclaimed for all to hear. All sorts of other people began putting questions to the hermit, always taking great care to make sure to ask for what they wanted anyway.

Having initially done his best to behave civilly to the newcomer, Uttam saw how the hermit's chest swelled when people addressed him as the Nameless One and how a little smile played round his lips when he remained mysteriously silent.

One day he went up to the hermit in the shrine, kneeling down before him. "Kanak here annoys me because he keeps displaying his carpets on top of my coils of rope. And his dog lifts his leg against the coils. I am going to slice up his carpets and then deal with his dog," he said, winking slyly out of the corner of his eye at Kanak. "Is this what I should do, oh Nameless One? If you don't speak, I will take that as a yes."

The hermit stayed calmly in the lotus position. Uttam went across to his stall and started sharpening one of the great knives he used to trim his rope ends. The dog made off but still the hermit didn't move a muscle. Bystanders began to laugh.

Uttam went up to the hermit. "Your silence annoys me. Since you don't use your tongue, I'm going to cut it out. Open your mouth!"

"You really shouldn't have done that," Neelam scolded him afterwards. "You even had poor Kanak alarmed. No wonder the hermit shouted out. Now people will always expect him to speak. It was better before, when people had to decide what they really wanted beforehand."

"He's a fraud," said Uttam defiantly. "Sitting there silently as though he were God. Shameless one, not nameless one, that's what he is."

"It's the people who want to make him into a god. They're the ones asking the questions. It's not his fault."

Two days later, Uttam tripped over one of his coils of rope and broke a leg. The hermit's reputation soared. More and more people came to see him in the shrine, taking special care how they asked their questions.

But most of the time they didn't find him in the shrine. Instead, they found him at Uttam's stall, shifting the heavy coils of rope and even delivering them when necessary to builders, passing boats and fishermen. He would use Uttam's cart to fetch the jute fibre needed for making the rope and do all sorts of other things which Uttam couldn't do. When Uttam's leg had healed, the hermit returned to the shrine. All the while he had not said a word.

Not long after, the hermit fell ill with fever. "God is punishing me," he moaned. Neelam made a bed for him out of a pile of Kanak's carpets. Jagadeep brought him light fish dishes, which the hermit was unable to eat, and Samir put up an awning to keep him dry when it rained.

But it was Uttam who saved the hermit's life, wiping his burning limbs with a cold, wet cloth and rubbing his body with strange herb potions. Day and night Uttam stayed by his side. The stallholders even sent for a doctor, at great expense, but he said that there was nothing more he could do than Uttam was already doing.

The fever reached crisis point. The hermit became delirious. Uttam kept applying cold compresses. He prayed to Durga. "He saved my business, now may his life be saved," he begged. Durga was silent.

The fever broke. It was clear that the hermit was going to live. Uttam performed cartwheels in the street and gave thanks to Dark Durga in the shrine.

"My body has been telling me something. I have been running away from life," said the hermit in a weak voice to Samir, with Uttam at his side. "You were right: I could never do enough. I was always pushing myself harder, always stripping away, thinking that there I would find the ultimate truth. Now, perhaps, the truth has found me. In fact, not even that matters. Who am I, that I am so important? What is important is the way that you all cared for me, especially Uttam.

"You have taught me that we are like one of your ropes," he went on. "Look." He picked up a stray piece of rope and took Uttam's villainous-looking knife. Cutting through the whipping cord at the end of the rope, he parted the strands with the tip of the knife. "This rope is made out of strand upon strand of jute. Take one strand and you can break it easily in your fingers, like this. But twist them all together and even a mad elephant could not break it. So also we must support one another, like you supported me. Perhaps now I may even be able to help you."

He tossed the piece of rope on the ground. "I too have learned from you," said Uttam. "People are not always what they seem. When you began giving yourself airs I thought you were like that other fellow, but you are not."

"You are right: it was beginning to go to my head. And I *was* like that other fellow. In fact, I used to *be* that other fellow. Amazing what shaving off your beard and a bit of politeness can do."

Sundar the Sitar Player

The young man carrying a sitar made his way slowly and shyly into the town of Prithura. He paused at the Palace gates and looked around. He was wondering whom he might ask to tell him the way, when he heard the clear, pure sound of a little wooden flute. The player, he saw, ran a pancake stall. In the quiet heat of the afternoon, he was playing the bamboo *venu* in the shade of an enormous magnolia tree with wonderful large white flowers.

The young man with the dusty feet and matted hair made his way over to the flute player. Vishnu, the pancake seller who had walked out of the Palace because it did not feel right to be king, looked up at the visitor. At a glance he could tell from the way the young man walked and was dressed that he had come a long way and that he was poor, even though he was wearing his best clothes. Vishnu smiled as he put his flute down on a box. "My new pineapple pancakes are the talk of the town!" he exclaimed.

The young man had not intended to have anything to eat but the smells were so delicious that he dug into his pocket for some money. Vishnu produced the largest pancake the man had ever seen and seemed to give him back almost more money in change than the young man had given him in the first place.

"I wonder if you can help me," said the young man. "My name is Sundar and I was looking for a sitar-maker I have heard of called Mahendra."

"Ah, Mahendra! He is one of most famous sitar-makers in all India – or at least he was, for he has all but retired now. I think he still makes the odd instrument, but not many." Vishnu was about to give him directions, but realised that the town was such a rabbit warren of streets that Sundar was bound to get lost. Reading his mind, his little daughter Tusti said brightly, "Let me take him, father! I know exactly where it is. Then I can play with Harinakshi."

Harinakshi was Mahendra's granddaughter. And so it was that little Tusti, who was just seven, led Sundar by the hand through the maze of streets. Picking their way between the stalls, carts, people, oxen and cows in the street, they eventually reached a tall house with, on the ground floor, a shop containing all sorts of musical instruments. Most were ones that Sundar had never seen before: bassoons, horns, a harp, clarinets and a grand piano. Tusti rang the bell and pushed open the door. A tall, elderly man with a ramrod-straight back and a magnificent long grey and white beard emerged from the back of the shop.

"My dear Tusti, I will tell Harinakshi you are here," he said.

"Oh good, she's home! Father has asked me to bring someone to you," she said, gesturing to the young man in his fine but faded clothes. And with that she scampered off into the house to find her friend.

"Since I was a little boy," said the young man hesitantly, "I have always loved playing stringed instruments. One day a passing musician gave me this sitar, but even he said that it was not very good and that I should need something better. I have come with all the money I have managed to save and am hoping that you might have something for me."

Mahendra looked at the young man. He supposed he was about seventeen. Like Vishnu, he could see that the young man had worn the best clothes he had for the occasion but even so could not escape the look of poverty. He glanced at the pitiful heap of coins that Sundar had emptied out of his pockets onto the table. It was hardly enough to buy so much as a single string for the cheapest sitar. But although strict and formidable looking,

Mahendra was also a kind man. He decided that he would let the young man try out one or two of his sitars, so that he would at least know what it was like to play a proper instrument. And then, gently, he would explain how much even the cheapest one cost and that it would take the young man many years of constant saving before he would be able to afford one.

"Try this one," he said. "Let us hear what you can do."

At first Sundar played hesitantly and nervously. Although a fine player, he had never explored his gifts to the full – perhaps because he had such a poor instrument. But even so, the humble instrument that Mahendra had taken down sprang to life under the young man's hands in a way that Mahendra would not have thought possible. Glorious sounds filled the room and people passing by the shop paused to listen.

Sundar stopped. "Wait, I have something better, try this," said Mahendra, disappearing into his workshop. He reappeared with a particularly fine looking white sitar. When he had tuned it he played a few notes and then gave it to Sundar. The young man again played for a few minutes, exploring every sound the magnificent instrument could play until it almost became a living thing. Mahendra held up his hand. "Wait! There is one other instrument I would like you to try."

Once again he disappeared into his workshop. This time he came back with a black sitar.

"This is something I made many years ago. When I had finished it I knew I had mastered my craft. Every other sitar I have made since then, including the white one, has been a variant on this one, but I have never managed to make such a fine one again. A number of musicians have made me handsome offers for it, but I have always refused, as I have never felt that they played it well enough."

Mahendra carefully and lovingly dusted it down. Silently, he handed it to the young peasant.

Even while Sundar was still tuning it the sitar seemed to strain forward and sing. When Sundar had finished tuning it, he stopped for a moment and closed his eyes. Then, with a sound like the rippling of water over rocks, he plucked a few of the strings with the lightness of a butterfly. Playing no more than a few simple notes, he managed to bring out riches and depths that had lain untouched in the great instrument since the time it was made. Slowly, the melody gathered pace and became more complicated. Now and then Sundar made mistakes, but it did not matter. From the sitar came the might of a thunderstorm, the sound of clashing armies, the smoothness of velvet and the tinkling of water on a marble fountain. It was as though the dazzling light of a thousand diamonds and emeralds exploded in the stuffy music shop. The sitar spoke to itself, backwards

and forwards, like two women gossiping, now laughing, now stern, now angry. The young man's fingers caressed from the twelve strings the hissing of a snake and the sighing of the wind in tall bamboo; he conjured up the sound of silk slipping from a shiny polished table, the crashing of waves on a rocky shore in the moonlight, the tiny sounds behind the stillness of a summer's day.

Mahendra listened to the mixture of exquisite happiness and delicate sadness until tears came to his eyes. The music reached a great climax in which he felt swept up in the sound like a child in the embrace of its mother. All things seemed possible as the musician's fingers sped up and down the neck of the instrument faster than the eye could follow: it was as though the very world and life itself were being opened up, as though nothing mattered anymore, as though all time beforehand had been leading to this point, and as though only he, the listener, knew exactly what it was that the great complexity of sound coming from the belly of the instrument was trying to convey.

And then, like a river crashing through mighty rapids, the music found its way back to the quietness of the original few notes. Sundar conjured up the sound of cicadas humming in the heat of the evening, mist gathering over a lake and dew drops settling on the grass.

When, at last, the final note had died away, the young man and Mahendra noticed Tusti and Harinakshi standing in the doorway, their faces filled with wonder. Mrs. Mahendra was there too, while the front of the shop was crowded with people. Sundar looked sadly at Mahendra. "I am afraid that my few coins are an insult," he said. "But one day, somehow, I will bring you the money."

"The sitar is yours," said Mahendra, with tears in his eyes. "Some things are beyond price. Take this sitar with my blessing into the world. It has found its rightful owner at last. I just ask that you come and play to these good people once a year."

Sundar was stunned. He held the sitar wonderingly in his hands. Wordlessly he stood up and embraced the old man.

Sundar gave his first public performance in the town that very day. Tusti led him back to Vishnu's pancake stall and the great banyan tree nearby. Against the backdrop of the tree's tall stilt-like roots, Sundar slowly began to make the sitar speak again. Suddenly, Tusti listened with astonishment to a new, utterly different sound: the hollow little boom and muffled explosion of the tabla drum. It was Mahendra. He did not play often, particularly now that he was old and has fingers had grown stiff. But now, like Sundar, he played like one possessed by angels. He and Sundar played as though they had been playing together all their lives. Now the sitar was not just in dialogue with itself but was chatting to the little drum. Their sounds would chase each other around like fish in a pond; the one would soar high while the other would sink low; now one would lead and then the other; they would chuckle, they would scold, they would laugh and dance and tumble over and over like dogs at play.

He returned to his village that night, reaching his home very late. His family woke up and, after hearing his story, begged Sundar to play a little for them too.

Sundar took the sitar out of its leather carrying case and just as he was about to begin playing found that the neck of the sitar was broken. The glue on the ancient instrument had dried out and the layers of wood had parted; perhaps his playing the previous day had been too much for it. A great feeling of sadness stole over him.

The next morning Sundar decided that the only thing was to take the instrument back to Mahendra. Perhaps he would be able to glue it.

The shadows cast by the sun were beginning to lengthen as Sundar entered the town. He wanted to slip unnoticed through the crowds and make his way to Mahendra's house, but people recognised him from the night before and almost dragged him to Vishnu's stall.

Vishnu listened with astonishment as Sundar told him about the broken sitar. "Mahendra died last night," Vishnu said softly.

Tusti and this time also Vishnu took Sundar through the winding streets. Mrs. Mahendra was at the door. She was dressed in white.

"He died at peace," she said. "Never before had he heard music like you played. The sitar he loved so much spoke through you. When he played with you it was as though the heavens opened for him. Now they have taken him back."

Sundar expressed his deep sorrow at Mahendra's death and decided he should not say anything about the cracked and useless sitar, which now lay in its leather case like a dead nightingale. But Tusti reached up and took Mrs. Mahendra by the hand and, with her wide eyes, said, "Mrs. Mahendra, the sitar broke last night! Sundar has come to have it repaired."

Mrs. Mahendra looked wonderingly at the sitar. "Its soul has flown, Tusti, like Mahendra's," she said at length. "It is enough that its true voice was heard once." As a fine musician herself, she feared the sitar would never be the same again, however carefully it was repaired. Besides, Mahendra had never been able to find a younger man to take over his craft.

She went to the back of the workshop and came back with the white sitar. "This is the most beautiful sitar my husband ever made, and he always said it was nearly as fine an instrument as the one he gave you. I know he would want you to have it."

Carefully Sundar placed the broken sitar on the workbench, covering it with a piece of embroidered blue silk that Mrs. Mahendra handed him.

On his way back he stopped under the banyan tree. He picked up the white sitar and repeated the few notes that Mahendra himself had played on it the day before: mournful and yet somehow, beneath the sadness, joyful sounds. He played with great gentleness and, as he played, became aware of a tabla being played too. The player was a local weaver, Rajani.

Sundar returned to his village that night. The next day he picked up the sitar, but the sounds he produced did not sound nearly as beautiful or magical to him as before. It was as though he had to learn how to play properly for the very first time. Sundar spent year after year of his life working on his technique. His dedication to his craft was legendary. He and Rajani were to play together for many years. They toured all over India and became so famous that they even performed in other countries. But each year, as Sundar had promised, they came back to the banyan tree and played for the people of Prithura.

Each time he would call on Mrs. Mahendra. One year she told him that she knew she, too, was dying. She asked Sundar all about his latest travels and his success and fame as a musician.

"I am only famous because of the inspiration your husband gave me through his sitar. But I have never played like that again. His soul was in that instrument, and sang through me. I may have mastered all the technique, but I know, and you know, that I am a mere maker of rough pots beside the master potter I was for that one day."

"Mahendra always said that he never sold that sitar because he never found anyone who truly loved it apart from me. I think it could sing again if you lovingly brought it back to life."

And with that the song of her own life came to an end.

Her words would not leave Sundar. One day not long after, he suddenly returned to Prithura. He was at the height of his fame, but more dissatisfied with his playing than ever. All his concentration on technique, he felt, had been at the expense of true feeling.

The workshop was still there. Sundar gave up performing and rented the workshop from the family. For many months he slowly learned the craft of making sitars, using Mahendra's old glues and tools and wood.

Then, at last, he knew the time had come. He had learned all there was to know. He removed the blue cloth from the black sitar.

The layers of wood were so badly curled and shattered that he had to work with great care, steaming the wood and then gluing it while it was still wet and soft with a special glue that dried and hardened slowly as the carefully clamped wood dried out. Layer after layer was lovingly added. In the meantime Sundar also worked on other instruments; the business was now as flourishing as it had been in Mahendra's day.

When, at last, the sitar was finished, Sundar eased his ageing limbs onto the mat and began to play. He realised how little he had been practising, and also that his fingers were becoming stiff with age. He knew the old sounds were there but, try as he might, he could produce no more than snatches and hints of its former glory.

Sadly, he put the instrument to one side. He would never be able to make it sing again.

Just then, a young woman with dusty sandals and carrying what Sundar could see was a homemade sitar shyly pushed open the door to the shop.

The Well

"Do I have to walk to the river again to fetch water?" complained eight-year-old Ila one morning. "Why is it that just the women have to fetch water? We are not as strong!"

In fact Ila quite enjoyed the walk through the fields and trees to the river through the lingering mist as the sun was rising and dew was still on the grass. She also enjoyed all the talk among the women as they filled their buckets from the great river. It was just that by the time they set off home the sun would be burning fiercely. And, although smaller than that carried by her mother, the bucket on her head seemed to grow heavier with each step. (Sometimes, when she thought no one was looking, she would give a little shake of her head so that some of the water slopped out. That would cool her off, lighten the load and, if she poured her bucket out quickly into the water tank when they got home, no-one would notice that it was not quite full.)

Her grandfather Manindra looked at her gravely. "Fetching the water has always been women's work," he said. "Besides, I am too old and, alas, your father has passed away."

"But what about Kanan?" she asked. Kanan was her elder brother. He was almost grown up.

"Kanan must look after the animals and often has to go to

market. He is also studying hard as he hopes one day to become a maths teacher."

But after she got back from fetching water Ila ran to find Kanan. He was milking the goats near some flame-of-the-forest trees. It was that time of the year when the trees were losing their leaves as their dazzling red flowers came out. "Why do I always have to fetch the water?" she demanded. "Sometimes we even have to go twice a day now."

"Dear Ila," said Kanan, "even the muddy water the animals drink is drying up now. So many factories are being built that take water from the river. The land is getting drier and drier."

"Why don't we dig a well?" she asked.

"Because it would cost far too much," Kanan explained. "The soil here is loose and sandy and the well would need to be properly lined with bricks."

But Ila's suggestion would not leave him. Life had become much more difficult since their father had died the year before, and now fetching enough water to meet their drinking needs and for the animals and the vegetable plot was draining the life out of the village. The older women accepted their lot but Ila, he felt, was quite right to protest, however gently.

So Kanan discussed the matter with his grandfather. Manindra had laid by a small sum of money but it was not nearly enough to build a well. Manindra, who was greatly respected, called a meeting of the village. All the people from Parsa came.

"Having a well would transform our village," Manindra said. "We could grow all sorts of fruit and vegetables and flowers and perhaps be able to sell some. Then we could even buy bicycles to take our produce to market more quickly. Think of all the time that our women would save and all the other things that they would be able to do."

Everyone agreed that a well would be a wonderful thing, and that they would rather be growing flowers than fetching water, but when they added up all the money they had between them it was still nowhere near enough. Parsa was a small, poor and remote village. It would cost a lot of money to have bricks and cement delivered and to get workers who knew how to build a well properly.

But Kanan was determined. "I will go to Prithura and try to borrow the money from a bank. I am sure they would understand that a well would be a good investment that would soon pay for itself."

After some discussion it was agreed that Kanan, who had such a good head for figures, should go. But there was also some grumbling. "How much will we have to pay each time we draw water from the well?" fat, elderly Prachi demanded to know, digging the woman sitting beside her in the ribs. "You'll see, that Kanan will get rich, just because all you younger women are too lazy to go to the river!"

"It will split the village," declared another woman. "We will be divided into haves and have-nots," she said, feeling very proud at repeating the expression she had heard on the radio - the village's one luxury.

"What if we dig the well and it turns out to be dry?" said one of the men. "We'll have spent a whole lot of money and just be having a hole in the ground."

But quiet, shy Amba surprised herself and everyone else by saying with great dignity and spirit that she had seen how her son Kanan had grown up into a man since her husband had so sadly been taken away from them and that she had every confidence he would do his best for the village and act fairly. Out of respect for the widow, it was agreed that Kanan should go to the town of Prithura.

Prithura was three days' walk away and it was further agreed that Kanan might take the one bicycle in the village. This was a sorry-looking, battered old machine, but at least it would greatly shorten his journey.

And so, wearing his best clothes, Kanan set off early one morning for Prithura. The air was fresh, the birds were singing and it felt good to be alive. Kanan pedalled off briskly. As he glanced back over his shoulder he could see little Ila standing on a mound and waving madly, until he rounded the

corner and Parsa disappeared from view.

Kanan sang as he pedalled along the little tracks beside the fields and through the forest. He made good progress. By late morning he was over halfway to Prithura, when all of a sudden the ride became very bumpy. Looking down he saw that he had a puncture. He had nothing to repair it with and the bicycle would be ruined if he kept trying to cycle along the uneven and

 stony tracks. Reluctantly Kanan hid the old bicycle in some bushes and continued on foot.

It was not until noon the next day that he reached Prithura. Kanan was tired, thirsty, hungry and dusty but he pressed on until he found a builder's merchant. He had done his sums carefully but the first thing he had to do was to make sure how much the well would cost.

"Oooh," said the merchant, rolling his eyes. "Parsa, you say. Never heard of it. No proper roads? Big difficulty. BIG difficulty. No electricity, now what about water? Ah yes, of course, that is why you are wanting a well. But if you have no water how will we mix the cement? So we will have to fetch water from the river."

The merchant's pencil flew backwards and forwards across his notebook. "Very difficult, very difficult, but I will give you a very good price, special price just for you."

The price was over three times as much as Kanan thought. Even after some hard bargaining the price was still far higher than he knew it should be, or than the village could afford.

He continued on his way.

The merchant ran after him shouting a lower price. But Kanan did not look back.

Eventually, after being quoted huge prices by one builder or merchant after another, Kanan at last found someone who seemed honest. He came from a village himself, understood the problem exactly and would do all he could to help. He came up with a price that was almost exactly what Kanan expected.

Just as they were about to shake hands on the deal, the man said, "For such a good price, of course I must be paid in full in advance." Although honest, Kanan was also shrewd. "I will pay you in advance for all the materials," he said, "but can only pay you for the transport and labour when the job is all done and the well is working properly." The man grew very excited and said that he was doing all he could to help and that Kanan would not find a lower price in all India. Once more, Kanan continued on his way.

By now Kanan was exhausted and in low spirits. He had come to the central part of the town, and slumped into a chair beside a pancake stall at the foot of the sloping Palace gardens. A young girl came up to him to take his order. She reminded him of his sister Ila.

"What's your name?" he asked, after ordering two apples pancakes.

"Tusti," she replied shyly.

"Why," Kanan exclaimed, "we have a Tusti in our village. She's a bit older than you and makes wonderful things out of flowers."

"What sort of things?" asked Tusti.

"Well, she makes garlands to put round your neck and she can even make animals like roosters and snakes out of flowers. She helps her mother to dry flowers and stick them onto paper to make beautiful greeting cards, which we sell at market."

"Oooh," said Tusti, "I'd like to see them. What's your village like?"

There was something so eager and trusting about the little girl that he quickly found himself telling her his story. She listened wide-eyed, totally forgetting to put the pancakes on.

Just then, Tusti's father Vishnu came up. "Papa, papa!" she said excitedly, "This man has come from a village where the women fetch the water and they need a well and a girl called Tusti just like me makes things out of flowers and he had a puncture and no-one will give him a fair price and he needs to find a bank to give him lots of money."

Vishnu smiled and bowed towards Kanan, hands folded in front of him. "You certainly look as though you have come a long way," he said kindly, as he started the pancakes cooking.

"I have, I have," said Kanan, returning the greeting. Once again he found himself telling his story. There was something about the stallholder too that made him feel he could trust him and he poured out his heart about all his hopes and difficulties.

The stallholder shouted to a rope seller several stalls along. "Uttam, you know a good builder, don't you?"

Uttam – a square-shouldered man with a magnificent long black beard - came over. Kanan had to tell his story all over again. His second, uneaten pancake grew cold and the stallholder put it back on the hotplate, quietly cooking an extra one as well. He set the plate before Kanan again.

Kanan's eyes grew wide. "I thought I had just eaten one of the pancakes, but now there are *still* two!" he exclaimed.

"That is how it works here," the stallholder said. "The more you eat the more apple pancakes appear on your plate. The charge stays the same, which is nothing, as you are our guest. But Uttam, you do know of a builder, don't you? Isn't there someone you often supply with rope for scaffolding?"

"There is," said Uttam. "His name is Rishabh. I can take you to him now."

The stallholder refused to accept payment and, in something of a daze, Kanan accompanied Uttam as they went in search of the builder.

They found him near the river, building a brick quayside and a wooden jetty. The sun was just setting and Rishabh was packing up his tools. Uttam explained that he had been sent by the pancake seller, Vishnu. Something stirred in Kanan's mind when he heard the name; he was sure that he had heard it before, but couldn't quite remember when.

Rishabh swung his legs over the brand-new quayside and invited the others to sit down beside him. He listened as Kanan told him about how his village needed a well and how he had been trying to get the work done at a proper price.

Rishabh took a piece of chalk and began doing some sums on the bricks. "How does that look?"

It was almost exactly equal to the figure that Kanan had in mind. They shook hands.

Kanan spent the night just outside the Palace railings on a sleeping mat that Uttam lent him. In the morning he breakfasted at the pancake stall, where Vishnu recommended a particular bank. He made his way to the town centre. Outside the ornate pillars of the Mercantile Bank of All India he dusted down his clothes as best he could and went inside. A fan flickered lazily from the ceiling. Everywhere he looked there was polished dark brown wood.

A bank clerk came up. Kanan said that he would like, if it were possible, to see the manager. The clerk replied haughtily: "You cannot just walk in off the street, you know. You need a letter of introduction or recommendation."

Kanan hardly thought that it would do to say that he had been given a recommendation by a pancake stallholder. On the other hand, the bank clearly was not going to do business with him, and he decided there was no reason to be ashamed of his new friend, who had shown him such respect and consideration. "A pancake seller near the Palace gates recommended that I should come here," he said simply, turning to go. To his astonishment, the bank clerk stiffened to attention and asked Kanan to follow him. At the end of a long gloomy corridor the clerk knocked on a large, impressive door. "It is not every day that we are sent someone by our former king!" he said as he swung open the door to reveal the manager sitting in his three-piece suit in a large swivel chair.

Mr Muckerjee bowed low and ordered an iced lime drink for his honoured guest. He displayed great interest in the village and the project. Rubbing his hands together, he said, "Now I am sure you have all the necessary paperwork."

"What sort of paperwork?" Kanan said hesitantly.

"Quotations, a builder's estimate, drawings, plans, that sort of thing." In his mind Kanan pictured the figures chalked on the brickwork. Even if they were still there, the bricks could hardly be dismantled and attached to his loan application form. When he explained that he had simply accepted a builder's word and shaken hands on the deal, the manager suddenly rose to his feet. He looked Kanan up and down, taking in the young man's somewhat odd, old-fashioned and still dusty clothes. "I am afraid we cannot commit our establishment's financial resources to a deal concluded in the backstreets of Prithura with some fly-by-night builder. Good day to you, sir."

Still reeling from the discovery that the kind pancake stallholder was in fact the former king - a story which now came back to him - Kanan stumbled through the streets of Prithura wondering what to do next. If the former king's recommendation had not been good enough for the Mercantile Bank of All India, it was unlikely that he would get very far with any other bank. And so it proved. On each occasion he was asked for the necessary paperwork and whether he himself would be able to put up a deposit of at least a quarter of the money required. Several times, he was sure, the burly Sikh bank guards with their colourful turbans would have thrown him out into the street if he hadn't made off smartly first.

By the end of the day, it was clear that his quest was hopeless. He would return to the village empty-handed. He did not want to go back to Vishnu and explain what had happened, as he thought that this might only embarrass him. His mind turned to the village and the line of women leaving each morning for the river; to the animal waterholes that were slowly drying up; to the cracks in the earth that were beginning to open up in the fields; and to the dust that found its way everywhere. Having a well would not solve all the problems, but would make life much easier.

In the park, Kanan found an empty bench. He rolled up his jacket to form a pillow and stretched out, but he could not sleep. His thoughts kept returning to the village, to all the builders and merchants he had bargained with, to the pancake stallholder and to all the banks that had made sure no money left their doors. Perhaps he should go to a moneylender? But he knew what they charged.

Being unable to sleep, he sat up again. At that moment, a well-dressed middle-aged man came round the corner and cut across the park. He was humming a lively tune. He passed Kanan, stopped, paused, and then turned back.

"Didn't I see you an hour or two ago, giving some money to a woman begging by the side of the street? I am sure it was you - you took such care giving her the money."

Kanan replied politely that it was.

"But I don't understand; now you almost look as though you yourself are begging."

"In a way," replied Kanan, "I suppose I have been begging all day, except not here but in banks!"

The man appeared not to be in any hurry. He sat down and asked Kanan to tell him his story.

When he was finished, the man was quiet for a while. Then he said: "I have been at the most expensive restaurant in town with some friends celebrating a big business deal. All this was made possible because many years ago a wealthy uncle gave me some money as a young man when my family was very poor. I invested the money in a small business and now it has grown into a large company.

"When my uncle gave me the money he said it was on condition that one day I too should give money to someone in need of a helping hand as they started out on life. He said that I would know when that day had come."

Reaching into his inside pocket he took out his wallet and handed Kanan twice the amount that he had said the well would cost. "Take this. When you build something it always costs more than you think at first. If there is any left over you can always buy bicycles for the village! And remember - one day you too must pass this gift on to someone else." Stammering his thanks, Kanan gave his assurance that he would do so. Whereupon the man vanished into the shadows of the night.

Kanan sat for some while on the bench. Then he got up and walked over to the woman sitting by the side of the park. He asked her what sum of money would change her life so that she no longer needed to beg. Startled, she mentioned a modest sum. Kanan took a few of the banknotes from his pocket, giving the woman twice what she had asked for. "If it had not been for you, good fortune would not have touched me as it has this night." And with that Kanan strode off in the darkness back to the village.

The Tin Mug

Mr Choudhury was a Very Important Person in the Indian Railways. He lived in a wide, leafy street in Bangalore, in a large, sprawling house with a spacious veranda. Every morning he would get on his bicycle and cycle to the Indian Railways office.

Mr Choudhury had a special passion in life. For as long as he could remember he had been looking for God but had never found God. But he knew that there were people who said that they had found God, and he wanted to meet one. If he could be sure, absolutely sure, that just one other person had met God, he would have that knowledge too and it would be the end of his quest.

His wife, Ranji, would tease him about his obsession. "Now, Kaviji, why is it that are you always reading books and trying to find someone who knows God? Can't you see God in the clouds and the trees and the flowers and the dew drops? Can't you find God within?"

But Mr Choudhury could not. Sometimes he would try to sit quietly and reflect on what he imagined to be God, but there were always weighty books to be read, talks to go to and, most of all, trips to be made in search of someone who was reported to have really glimpsed God.

Now there are many very holy people in India. Because of his job as an inspector, Mr Choudhury had to travel all over India. Wherever he went he would make inquiries about local holy men and women. Sometimes he would take extra leave so that he could visit them, as some of them lived in remote places that were not easy to reach.

Each time, however, Mr Choudhury came away disappointed. He found that when he really questioned people closely they knew God no more than he did. He met many extraordinary people. He met fakirs who could be buried alive for days without food and water, slow their bodies right down, and emerge again as though nothing had happened. He met snake-charmers and magicians, and people who could sit cross-legged on a rock for days on end in meditation. He met hermits who lived in caves for years and years.

Once he even climbed a mountain to meet a woman who had lived up there all by herself for eighteen years. Every spring when the snows melted a donkey would be sent up with food supplies for the next year. Mr Choudhury volunteered to escort the donkey. "Don't you get lonely and bored?" he asked the woman. She told him that she felt in touch with all the woes of the world and had never been busier praying to make sure that all would be well. But do you know God, he asked? God is in the mystery, God is beyond knowing, she said.

Mr Choudhury went away disappointed.

Mrs Choudhury told him to keep looking for God in the scarlet and gold of a butterfly's wing, in the patient gaze of a cow and in dust particles caught in a shaft of sunlight in the corridor. Mr Choudhury told her to keep dusting.

One day Mr Choudhury came back from work on his bicycle. It was a hot day and he was perspiring. He took off his jacket, loosened his tie and slumped into a wicker chair on his veranda. He had just poured himself a large, ice-cold lime drink and smoothed out the folds in the newspaper, when a man who was surely a beggar appeared before him. The few cloths draped around his body were ragged and dirty. "Would you be kind enough to give me a glass of water?" said the man, holding out a battered old tin mug. Mr Choudhury looked at him suspiciously and motioned without speaking in the direction of the kitchen. The man slipped away.

Mr Choudhury felt guilty and a bit cross with himself that he hadn't given his delicious lime drink to the man. It would have been a kind gesture. Who knows what the man's story was. But it was too late now.

Some time later he saw the man make his way down the drive and out the gate into the street with its golden acacias and magnificent blue jacaranda trees. Moments later Mr Choudhury's dear daughter Sarita burst through the glass-panelled front door and came running onto the veranda. "Did you speak to him, father?" she asked. "He said that he knew someone in his village who knows God! A very modest man hardly anyone knows about."

Mr Choudhury sprang to his feet. "I must find him!" he exclaimed. Leaping onto his bicycle he sped down the drive, the tyres spitting stones, and out into the road. The beggar was nowhere to be seen. He cycled up and down all the side streets until, in exhaustion, he finally made his way to the park to get a drink of water from the fountain.

Children were playing football with a tin can. In fact, it was more a game of hide and seek. Whoever was "it" would put the can on the ground and, while he was trying to find the others, someone would dash out from behind the bushes and kick the can away before the person who was "it" could catch them. As Mr Choudhury rode up on his bicycle he could not resist swerving onto the grass and, wobbling because of his considerable weight, giving the can a mighty kick with his heavy leather shoe. The can sailed through the air, scattering a group of ducks by the pond. The children shouted and protested that Mr Choudhury was spoiling the game.

Panting, Mr Choudhury lent his bicycle against a tree and slumped onto a bench. What was wrong with him? He had been unkind to a poor beggar and interfered with the children's game; it was no wonder he couldn't find God.

He felt a light touch at his elbow. Being held before him was an old, battered tin mug full to the brim with water. Recognising the mug he sprang up – to find the beggar. "I – you – I have been looking for you everywhere!" he exclaimed. "You see, well, it's just, well - my daughter tells me that you know a man who knows God!"

"I do," said the man quietly. "He is the Sage Who Never Speaks."

"The sage who never speaks? Never speaks? What good is that to anyone? How then do you know that he knows God?"

"You would have to meet him, then you would know. Everyone knows from his loving kindness that he truly knows God. He used to speak, but now he only occasionally writes on a blackboard. He always says: 'You must lose what you never had, to find what you never lost'."

Mr Choudhury looked in astonishment at this beggar speaking in mysterious riddles. After draining the mug, he remembered uncomfortably how he had failed to get the beggar some water earlier that very day. To make amends he went over to the fountain to fill the tin mug for him.

When he came back the beggar had vanished.

Mr Choudhury hastily struggled back onto his bicycle and criss-crossed the park at high speed. The beggar was nowhere to be seen. The light was fading. Eventually, lost in thought, he cycled back home.

By now the creamy white flowers on the frangipani trees lining the drive were gleaming in the dusk like soft lanterns. Mr Choudhury slumped into his chair, pondering on the strange events.

His daughter Sarita came out again through the glass-panelled door. "Did you find him?" she asked.

"I did, but then I lost him again. He vanished, vanished just like that into thin air. He told me about the Sage Who Never Speaks, but I didn't even have time to ask him where he lives."

"Oh, he said something to me about where he lived. Let me

think now, yes, he said that the sage lived in a village an hour from, where was it now, yes – Prithura, I'm sure he said Prithura."

Now Prithura was a long way from the city in which Mr Choudhury lived. Luckily, however, he was able to decide that an urgent inspection of the branch railway lines in Prithura was required. He also took a few days extra leave. His wife scolded him as she packed his neatly ironed shirts into his little suitcase. "Kaviji, Kaviji, going off again, on your wild goose chase. Always reading, always searching, always looking without seeing."

"This is different, this is different! You know, I am sure I have heard of this Sage Who Never Speaks before. I think I may have read about him in one of my books. 'You must lose what you never had, to find what you never lost.' I wonder what he meant by that."

"Ah well, I can only hope you find the man. It would be such a relief if your quest were over. But why you think that an old man in raggedy clothes who speaks in riddles can help you find someone who truly knows God I do not understand."

Mr Choudhury listened good-naturedly to his dear wife, reflecting that she simply did not understand how important it was to be in the presence, just once in his life, of someone who had glimpsed God. He strapped his suitcase to his bicycle, said goodbye to Ranji and Sarita, and pedalled off to the railway station.

In Prithura Mr Choudhury made many enquiries but no one seemed to know of the Sage Who Never Speaks. Taking buses and hiring a bicycle he gradually visited all the villages within an hour of Prithura, but still he could not find the sage. At last, exhausted, he flopped down under an enormous banyan tree, propping his bicycle up against the strange stilt-like roots. He would have to go back to Prithura, catch the train back home and face more gentle teasing by his wife.

Suddenly, he felt a sense of total despair and emptiness. It was as though the life had drained out of him. He had been searching for so, so long, all to no avail. He thought of all the journeys he had made, the countless people he had met, the ceremonies and rituals he had attended, all the wisdom he had sought to glean from books. He was no wiser than when he began. He was wasting his time. It was time to go home. Tears ran quietly down his cheeks and his body shook with sobs.

Just then a small boy playing with a football came up to him. "Are you all right?" the boy asked kindly. "You look so sad."

Coming back to reality with a start, Mr Choudhury decided that it would be too complicated to explain everything to such a small boy. Trying to smile, he simply said, "An old friend of mine has died. A bit like a twin brother, someone who has always been with me."

The boy seemed to understand, or at least didn't ask any further questions. Mr Choudhury asked the boy his name and where he lived. He replied that he was called Sasha and lived in a village at the top of the hill.

"Would you like to play football? I'll be goalie."

Mr Choudhury struggled to his feet. Two of the stilt-roots made an excellent goal and Mr Choudhury tried to drive shots past Sasha. Although he was quite portly, Mr Choudhury could kick the ball surprisingly hard and Sasha's hands stung. "Wow, you're good," he said. "My friends can't kick the ball as hard as you."

"You're good too," said Mr Choudhury. "You're like a human crackerjack, jumping this way and that!"

They laughed. Just then it began to rain: big, fat, warm drops of rain. They sheltered under the tree but soon the water began working its way through the leaves. Then Mr Choudhury remembered that he had a little foldaway umbrella in his saddlebag. With Mr Choudhury wheeling his bicycle with one hand and holding the umbrella in his other hand over them both, they slowly trudged up the long hill together.

They walked in silence. In any case, it was raining so hard that it was almost impossible to make oneself heard. As they reached the top of the hill the rain began to ease. "That's where I live," said Sasha, pointing down a lane. "But if you want to stay dry, you could go into that temple over there, and see the man who never speaks. He's weird."

"Man who never speaks?" stammered Mr Choudhury.

"Yes, he's been there for ever so long. I and my friends go and watch himself sometimes, just for fun. Now and then he writes things on a blackboard."

"What sort of things?" said Mr Choudhury, catching his breath.

"Oh, strange things like - like about giving things up and losing them because you didn't ever have them anyway – I don't really understand it. I think he's a bit of a nut-case but I quite like him because he looks at you in such a kind way. Hey, I'll go in with you if you like."

Mr Choudhury leant his bicycle against the fence and they went up to the gate. There was a young man there. "Ha, Sasha, my little friend. Brought someone to meet the Master, have you? Do please go in, sir. The Master is inside."

"Who's that?" whispered Mr Choudhury.

"He's an alokite," said the boy gravely. "He's called Girish."

"I think you mean an acolyte," said Mr Choudhury. "Someone who's a follower – a bit like a football supporter with a special pass."

"Yes, that's it," said Sasha, putting his ball down on the grass. "Hey, Girish, will you look after my ball?" he called out loudly over his shoulder.

"Shhh," said Girish, lifting his finger to his lips and pointing to the temple.

Sasha laughed and skipped ahead, leading Mr Choudhury up to the temple door. They went inside.

Sitting around were 20 or so more acolytes, in their unbleached cotton robes. In the middle of the room was a slightly elevated dais, with on it a heavy wooden chair. Sitting on the chair was - the beggar from the park.

Mr Choudhury looked at him in astonishment. "You - you cannot be the same man. You are deceiving me! You cannot be the Sage Who Never Speaks, for when I saw you just a few days ago you spoke! Your words to me were…"

"That you must lose what you never had, to find what you never lost," said the Sage Who Never Speaks.

A gasp went up from the acolytes. The Sage had spoken!

The Sage went on, "You have done the first half, but have still to do the second."

Mr Choudhury looked again at the Sage. He was sure it was the same man. His voice was the same, he still talked in riddles and he looked the same, except that he was wearing a saffron-coloured robe instead of his ragged beggar's garments.

Taking the boy by the hand, Mr Choudhury hurried back outside to collect his wits. There, they found Girish keeping the ball up in the air with his feet, knees and head. He quickly gathered in the ball, and asked if they had seen the Sage.

"Yes, but he must be an impostor! Just two days ago I saw him in Bangalore, dressed as a beggar. I don't understand how he could have got back so quickly, or why he spoke to me when he never speaks."

"Are you sure it was the same man?"

"Yes! Look, he even left behind this old tin mug."

Girish started. "But that is the mug he has lost and we have all been looking for."

"Well then, give it back to him," said Mr Choudhury, handing the battered object to Girish.

"But you don't understand," said the acolyte. "The Master has been here every single day for the last week. He never leaves here."

Two days later, Mr Choudhury was back at the Railway Station in his home town. It was late in the evening. He found his bicycle where he had left it and pedalled slowly home, lost in thought. However would he explain to Ranji and Sarita what had happened? And in any case, what did it all mean?

He came to his house and cycled up the drive, past the frangipani trees with their ghostly white flowers. He put his bicycle away and climbed the steps to the veranda. With a shock, he saw the features of the beggar in the glass-panelled front door.

As he drew closer, he realised that the face was his own.

The Stranger at the Shrine

Day after day the stranger went up to the shrine to Dark Durga. There was something unusual about him: a mixture of intensity and simplicity. No one knew who he was and yet some people said that he seemed familiar to them.

Sometimes he would spend a few minutes at the shrine; sometimes he would stay for several hours. Sometimes his eyes would be closed and sometimes they would be open, but always he was totally still. He walked slowly and a little awkwardly, and had an unusually fine, unmarked complexion.

Late one afternoon the mysterious stranger came when it was raining heavily. He did not stay in the shrine for long. As he was leaving, his foot slipped on the wet steps and he fell heavily to the ground. Most of the stallholders had packed up because of the rain, but Samir was still there and ran over to pick him up. Even with Samir's help, the man had difficulty getting to his feet. At last, swaying unsteadily in the rain, he thanked Samir with great courtesy.

"Come, sit down under my awning here," said Samir. "You have taken a nasty fall and need to rest a while. I will send for some tea."

Samir signalled to a small boy who was playing barefoot in the puddles and handed him a coin. The boy scampered off to Vishnu's stall and returned not just with a beaker of tea, but with a pineapple pancake as well.

"I told my father the man had fallen over and that you were looking after him and that he was hurt and here was some money for some tea and dad said take the tea but he will want something to eat as well," the boy explained as raindrops bounced off the pancake and created little fountains in the tea.

"Thank you, Loprakesh," said Samir gravely, trying not to smile. But the man laughed. "You're quite a runner, aren't you?" he said kindly. "Just as well, or the tea would be all rainwater by now!" He poured the tea from the beaker into a battered tin mug, which appeared to be his only possession.

"Tell me, how old are you, Loprakesh?"

"Six."

"Ah, a very fine age. And what do you want to be when you grow up?"

"An engine-driver," Loprakesh replied.

"Oh, well now, I know a story about an engine-driver," said the stranger. And he told Loprakesh about an engine-driver with the most powerful locomotive in all India, the steam from which would billow up into the sky to form vast white clouds.

"But the driver got tired of always being stuck to the rails. One day he decided to attach vast wings to his great steam-engine so that it could fly. When the job was done the locomotive soared into the air and the engine-driver towed his train right across the sky like a great flock of birds. When he couldn't find anywhere to land he parked his train in a big black cloud."

The man paused for a moment after a flash of lightning.

"And the sound we call -," he said, just as there was a loud roll from the heavens, "THUNDER!! is the sound of the engines and the carriages riding along the bumpy clouds!"

Loprakesh laughed. "Do you know any more stories?"

The rain was continuing to fall. It drummed on the tin roofs of nearby shanty dwellings and at times was so heavy that it was almost impossible to hear oneself speak. The man looked at Loprakesh's eager young face. Slowly he told him a legend about a silversmith who was so engrossed in working on a beautiful goblet that he did not notice when the king was passing by and was nearly put to death for failing to show respect.

Samir saw how moved the stranger was by his own story, and glanced at him wonderingly. He wanted to ask who he was, but the man had a certain calm reserve and an air of sadness and mystery that held Samir back from saying anything. Loprakesh, however, looked at the man wide-eyed. As the rain eased, he said, "Please, sir, what is your name, and where have you come from?"

The man smiled. "My name, Loprakesh, is Vishivas. Do you know what the name means?"

Loprakesh shook his head. "No, but it sounds a bit like my father's name. He's called Vishnu. That's him over there, at the pancake stall, by the Palace fence. What does it mean?"

"It means trust."

"Trust!" exclaimed Loprakesh. "That's a strange name."

"It is indeed. People would tease me about it when I was your age, reminding me of my name whenever I did anything wrong or silly. After everything that has happened to me it is even stranger that it should be my name."

It was not what Vishivas had meant to say, but there was something so innocent about Loprakesh that the words had popped out before he realised.

"What did happen to you?"

Vishivas paused. For a moment it seemed as though he would retreat into his own world but, once again, he looked at Loprakesh's eager face, and he knew too that Samir could be trusted.

"Was that silversmith someone you knew?" Loprakesh pressed him.

Vishivas looked startled. "In a way, he was," he replied. "You see – well, I have just been released after twenty-five years in prison."

Samir and Loprakesh fell silent, staring at the stranger

"So that is why I come to the shrine every day, to give thanks for that time."

"For having been in prison? Surely – surely you come to give thanks for your freedom?" stammered Samir.

"Yes, for that too," replied Vishivas. "I know it seems strange, but I am grateful for all those years in prison. You see, when I was a young man I led a dangerous and foolish life. My parents had died when I was young, I did not go to school and I fell in with a gang of boys and young men who were up to no good.

"The details don't matter, but one day there was a big fight and one of our group ended up being stabbed. Everyone ran away except me. I tried to save him but he died in my arms. When the police came there was blood all over my clothes and the knife was lying by my side. I was arrested and placed on trial. The authorities were fed up with our gang and didn't care whether I was the one who had done it or not. They wanted to make an example of me.

"Within a few days I was taken to court. I was terrified, although I tried not to show it. The trial did not take long. I was found guilty. At the end the judge sentenced me to death. I collapsed and was carried down to the dungeons.

"I was told that I would be executed the next morning. Needless to say I didn't sleep that night. I threshed about and paced up and down my wretched, slimy cell. The night was at its darkest. I was at my lowest point. And then, well, it's hard to explain, but all of a sudden my cell was flooded with light. It was a light and yet it was not a light; it was a light that I could see, but also couldn't see; and it was outside me but also inside me. The guard sitting on a stool outside the cell didn't notice anything.

"When the sensation of the light had faded, I could still feel it inside me. Indeed, I can to this day. I somehow knew that all would be well; I knew that whatever happened to me, Vishivas, no longer mattered.

"The execution was set for midday. Shortly after dawn, the guard opened my cell and marched me in chains to the prison gates. 'Where are we going? Surely it isn't time yet?' I asked. The guard opened the gates and said, 'You have been summoned by the King'. That is all he would say.

"I thought that this must be the custom before an execution. I was brought before King Raman. Queen Pari was by his side."

Loprakesh jumped up and was about to say something but Samir put his hand on his arm and Vishivas continued, without noticing anything.

"I remember thinking that they both looked tired and pale-faced. Avoiding my eye, the King asked me if I had anything to say for myself.

"'Only,' I replied, 'that I did not kill my friend, and that I am at peace. You must do what you have to do.'

"The King looked startled. The beautiful and graceful Queen looked at me directly and with great kindness; I felt the same stillness that had entered my cell. She whispered into the King's ear. I just caught a few words – 'surely', 'show pity', 'our daughter's birthday'. The King looked confused and angry. He dismissed me with a wave of the hand. I was taken back to the dungeons. Later that morning, I was told the King had decided to show me mercy. I was not to be killed but would spend the rest of my life in prison."

Again Samir restrained Loprakesh, putting a finger to his lips. "I cannot imagine how difficult it must have been for you, an innocent man," he said. "It would have left me very bitter."

"Well, you see, I was, but I also was not, innocent. Had I continued to behave as I was as a young man, even worse things would have happened. I would probably be dead now. In the beginning, it is true, it was very difficult. I was filled with rage and despair. The experience had taken me so low that I had to reach up to touch bottom. But then I would always return to that sense of peace. One day, it dawned on me that I had to make the best of my life, even in a place such as that.

"I learnt too that the monsters I thought inhabited the dungeons were human beings. They shared what little food they had with me. They looked after me when I fell ill. There were even one or two who could read and write, and they taught me to read and write too. I learned that I was not alone in receiving a strength from beyond myself, and that many of those there had already been punished dreadfully by life long before they ever came to prison.

"The years went by. Some of the prisoners I came to know, and even love, died; others were released. New people were flung into the dungeons, whom I tried to help as best I could.

"After spending so many years underground in damp and squalid conditions, I eventually grew weak. My throat rattled when I breathed. The Governor of the prison ordered that I should be placed in a separate cell, above ground. All I had was a stone slab on which to sit and sleep, but the air was fresh and my bare surroundings felt like unimaginable luxury.

"High up in one wall was a slit-shaped window. Although it was narrow, I would sit for hours watching the passing clouds

and the occasional bird during the day, while at night I could see
the stars go slowly by and catch a glimpse of the moon.

"One day, a frangipani blossom that had been lifted up in the
wind came tumbling in through the window.
It was creamy and smooth, and I thought it
was the most beautiful thing I had ever seen.
Its fragrance filled the cell for days, until it
slowly turned brown and shrivelled up.

"My health improved. Some of the
guards were kind. The Governor would come
to see me and would sometimes talk for a
while. I was brought things to read and given
proper food. Even so I missed my companions
- those monsters in the dungeon.

"One morning, the Governor came to
my cell and unlocked the barred door. 'You
are free,' he said.

"'Free?' I exclaimed. 'Whatever can you mean?'

"'Last night, a wealthy and famous businessman who
lay dying insisted that he be carried through the streets on a
stretcher to see the Chief Justice. With his last few words he
told the Chief Justice that it was he, not you, who had killed that
young man all those years ago. He did not want to die with the
secret in his heart.

"That was a few days ago. I have been coming to this
shrine every day since then to give thanks. Durga, you see, is
the goddess who brings everything together. She embraces the
darkness and shows the way through.

"I come to give thanks to her. What I would also dearly like
is to give thanks to King Raman and Queen Pari for showing me
mercy, but I cannot think of any way in which I might manage
to see them."

The words had barely left his mouth before Loprakesh was
scampering off towards the Palace fence. Vishivas looked up in
alarm. "Oh dear," he said, "perhaps my story was too much for
him." But Samir just smiled and said "Wait!"

They watched as in the distance Loprakesh jumped up and
down tugging at his father's sleeve. Something he said made
his father pause. He called over his wife. Even at a distance,

Vishivas could see how beautiful and graceful she was. She reminded him of someone.

The three of them came back to Samir's basket stall beside the shrine. When Samir bowed before her, Vishivas realised all at once that this must be Princess Savitri, the daughter of Queen Pari.

"Samir," said Savitri with mock sternness, "you know I have told you never to bow." She turned to Vishivas. "Now, Loprakesh, what is it that you were going to say to our friend Vishivas?"

"Come and meet Grandpa and Grandma!" he shouted gaily, tugging at Vishivas's hand. "Tell them the story about the king and that man making the globule."

Later, as the head of a famous ashram, Vishivas would often be asked to tell the story of the silversmith and the goblet.

The Silver Goblet

Once, long ago, a silversmith was sitting at his bench working at a silver goblet. The enormous goblet was for presentation to the king, who was to visit the town later that day. The silversmith was working hard to finish it in time for the visit. He was busy engraving the bowl and foot with the most superb designs and pictures: it traced the course of a river from source to the sea, with beside it elephants, monkeys, goats, rose bushes and swaying bamboo fronds, and much else besides. He was utterly absorbed in his work; his engraving pen had almost taken on a life of its own.

So engrossed was the silversmith in adding the final, intricate scrolls and decorations that he did not even notice when the king arrived early and rode into the town at the head of a long line of courtiers and soldiers. The streets were thronged with people lifting their hats and cheering.

As the procession passed the silversmith's workshop, a soldier of the guard noticed that the silversmith had not stood up as the king passed. Striding into the workshop he demanded in a loud voice to know why the silversmith had remained seated. "Have you no respect for the king?"

The silversmith did not even look up but, moving the goblet slightly in his hands so that it caught the shaft of light coming in through the window, continued working on the final scroll. The soldier dashed the goblet from his hands and hauled the silversmith to his feet. "You shall stand in the presence of your king!" he roared.

The soldier clapped the silversmith in irons and dragged him off to the Captain of the Guard. "This man has insulted His Majesty!" he declared.

The Captain of the Guard took the silversmith to the Lord Chancellor. When he had heard the story the Lord Chancellor declared loudly, "Erect a gallows and have this miserable man executed at sunset."

As the last rays of sunlight turned the brickwork pink, the queen, inside the building, caught the sound of a long, menacing drum roll. She asked the king anxiously what it was. He beckoned over a courtier to find out what was happening. When he had been told, the king exclaimed, "Bring the man to me!"

With great haste a page scampered down the corridor, hurled himself down the steps, sprinted across the courtyard and reached the gallows just as the rope was being placed over the silversmith's head.

The silversmith was brought before the king. "What have you to say for yourself?" demanded the king.

"Sire," said the silversmith, looking at the king evenly, "I was working on a silver goblet that was to be presented to you on this happy day, but was so absorbed in my work that I did not even notice you pass. It was as though Shiva Himself had entered into the very silver and the engraving pen."

The king was silent. At length he said, "Fetch me the goblet."

A member of the guard was sent to retrieve the goblet. It was placed before the king on a small, high table covered with a red velvet cloth. The goblet sparkled and gleamed in the light of the many candles and the rising moon.

The king marvelled at the intricacy and beauty of the design. His eye was led round the goblet, from the bubbling spring in the mighty mountains to the water tumbling down the rocks, from the river gliding through the plains to the swishing seas, from the stars at night to the dew of the dawn. It was as though he could hear the wind in the trees, smell the scent of the white roses and taste the salt on the sea air.

"And what would you have done if the Lord Shiva himself had appeared before you at the bench?"

The silversmith thought for a moment and then replied: "I should have continued with my work. What could I do with a god before me? I could speak to the god, I could touch the god, I could even hug the god, but a god outside me would be less real than the god I have and know and love inside me, and who is with me in my work, and whom I see in you."

There was a long silence. Then, kneeling down, the king held the goblet out in his cupped hands for the silversmith to drink, and set him free.